THE WIND HOWLED ACROSS

the open fields and whistled through the tombs. In the distance, I could hear the thundering of hooves.

The magic trembled in me, flew around me, pulled at the world, and drew what I would from it. We stood and chanted the old words, words of power, until our voices grew hoarse and our throats were raw. At last we stopped.

Abruptly, the air was still and silent. I released Caimbeul's hand and turned. Below us, at the base of the hill where the cairns stood, was the Hunt.

Black fur melted into black night. At their head was a tall, cloaked form. A long, bony arm appeared from the depths of the apparition's cloak. I glanced at Caimbeul. His lips were set in a hard line.

"You don't have to come," I said.

"What?" he replied. "And miss all the fun?"

SHADOWRUN

WORLDS WITHOUT END

Caroline Spector

A ROC BOOK

ROC
Published by the Penguin Group
Penguin Books USA Inc., 375 Hudson Street,
New York, New York 10014, U.S.A.
Penguin Books Ltd, 27 Wrights Lane,
London W8 5TZ, England
Penguin Books Australia Ltd, Ringwood,
Victoria, Australia
Penguin Books Canada Ltd, 10 Alcorn Avenue,
Toronto, Ontario, Canada M4V 3B2
Penguin Books (N.Z.) Ltd, 182-190 Wairau Road,
Auckland 10, New Zealand

Penguin Books Ltd, Registered Offices:
Harmondsworth, Middlesex, England

First published by Roc, an imprint of Dutton Signet,
a division of Penguin Books USA Inc.

First Printing, October, 1995
10 9 8 7 6 5 4 3 2 1

Series Editor: Donna Ippolito
Cover: Peter Peebles

RoC REGISTERED TRADEMARK—MARCA REGISTRADA

Foreword

There has always been magic. And magic has a life of its own. It comes and goes without our control. It flows through the world as it will.

This is how the world was Awakened.

Magical energy ran through the veins of the world like blood through humans. It changed her. And it changed her people.

And it came to pass that events shaped by magic began to alter history.

Earthquakes tore the earth apart. The Four Horsemen of the Apocalypse seemed to be riding across the world. Conquest, War, Famine, and Death raged unabated. The VITAS plague alone took almost a quarter of the world's population in the year 2010.

Then came 2011: the Year of Chaos.

Governments fell. Famine gripped the poor and stalked the wealthy. Nuclear power failed, causing massive radiation fallout. War peppered the world, toppling heads of state, creating new countries.

And then there were the children.

At first, they were called deformities. Then mutations. The superstitious called them changelings, and saw the Hand of God at play. Finally, science offered a label: UGE. Unexplained Genetic Expression. Everywhere you looked the media ran stories about these babies, calling them elves and dwarfs. The age-old specter of prejudice had found new victims.

At the end of 2011, the most dramatic event of the newly Awakened world occurred. The great worm, Ryumyo, rose from his long sleep inside Mt. Fuji. Thousands watched as the first dragon the technological world had seen took to the sky. In dragon fashion he ignored humans. Humanity got its first close-up look at a dragon when Dunkelzahn consented to a series of trideo interviews. The ratings were fantastic and launched Dunkelzahn as an international celebrity.

In 2014, The Native American Nations claimed responsibility for the eruption of Redondo Peak. This cataclysmic event buried nearby Los Alamos in volcanic ash. In a desperate measure to assert control, the United States government sent federal agents in to stop the NAN uprising. They were swept into oblivion by tornadoes resulting from the powerful shamanistic magic of the Great Ghost Dance.

After this, the changes in the world began to happen at a faster and faster pace. There was the so-called goblinization of 2021. Overnight, people began to change into fantastic creatures once thought to exist only in fairy tales. The stuff of legend.

And buried deep within the Awakening was a mystery from the past.

A time so far away from present events that only a handful of people knew the truth.

About how the world once was. And how it might become again.

When magic was as much a part of life as breathing, or eating, or seeing, or feeling. And how the world was made full of heroes and troubadours, and mages, and wild things the modern world could not fathom. And how the very magic that flowed through this world also drew the greatest evil to it.

And when that evil came for the people, one great race understood the futility of fighting this new plague upon the land. The Theran Empire promised a way to survive the hundreds of years this Scourge would last. They sent the people of the world into deep underground kaers where they would live magically sealed against the invaders until the time when they could come back to the surface again.

But such generosity of vision always has its price.

However, that is another story.

And now we have come back again to the magic. And to those who would guard the world from the horrors of the past.

Those who have lived through it all before.

Prologue

Let me tell you a story . . .

Once upon a time there was a woman.

Sometimes, in the story, her name is Pandora. Sometimes it's Eve. And sometimes it's Lilith.

There are more names for her.

It all depends on who's telling the story.

At any rate, at one time everything in the world was wonderful. Or so you're supposed to believe. There was enough food for everyone to eat. Enough water to drink. No one had to work.

In short: Paradise.

Except for one thing.

The woman.

You see, in this story she's at the root of all the trouble.

Either she can't help opening the box. Or talking to the snake. Or she's just too uppity for her own good.

And she starts poking around in things. Things We Were Not Meant to Know. And as a result, everything goes to hell in a handbasket.

Or so the person telling the tale would have you believe.

Of course, since everything in the world isn't total drek, there has to be some sort of mitigating factor.

Like we're banished from the garden. But, if we work and pray hard enough, we might be let back in. Or we're told that the woman was banished to the edge of time and there she mated with demons. And her offspring come to us in our dreams and torment us.

Seduce us.

Lead us astray.

And then, in some versions of the tale, at the bottom of the box is Hope. Which, we're told, is the only way to survive all the other horrors which have already escaped from the box. It is the only thing we have to hold on to.

Or so we're told.

But that's the way it is with stories.

You just don't know who you can trust.

PART I

"Oh fuck, not another elf!"

—Hugo Dyson, during the reading
of a manuscript by J.R.R. Tolkien

Across the frozen planes of time I've come. Through fires brighter than a thousand suns. Through darkness. Through the Void. Over the range of the universe I've come.

I've come for you, Aina.

To take you again into my sweet embrace and show you wonders from the darkness of your soul. Then I'll make you yearn for death while I rip open your mind and lay waste to everything you hold dear.

But all that will come later. For we have centuries, no, millennia to play our games. Come to me now and let me show you ... let me show everything I have to offer.

1

Last night I dreamt again of Ysrthgrathe.

And when I awoke, the stench of death and corruption still lingered in the air.

Through my bedroom window moonlight poured cold and blue. I rubbed my eyes, trying to convince myself that it had only been a dream. That the demons lurking in the shadowed corners were in my imagination. A conjuring of my mind only.

I shoved the covers away, letting the night air

send gooseflesh across my arms and down my legs. Here by the sea on the northern coast of Scotland the weather stays chill and damp all year long. It had never bothered me before. But tonight, I felt the cold straight to my bones. *All the better to keep me awake,* I thought.

My feet shrank as they touched the cold bare floor. Grabbing my thick robe, I wrapped it tightly about me. It was made of real, heavy, woven cashmere fabric, not that horrid synth stuff they sell nowadays.

I went downstairs and made myself some tea. It warmed my body, but I still felt chilled. I wanted to read, but I hated using the foul contraption Caimbeul had given me. The vidscreen gave me a headache and I could never bring myself to have cyberware implanted. Bodmod, cyberjunk, ticklewires—whatever they're calling them this week.

Hadn't I done enough of that sort of thing to myself in the past?

I shuddered as I thought about Ysrthgrathe.

Too soon, I thought. *It's too soon.*

But I knew it wasn't. The very thing I'd sought to prevent seemed to be happening. That is, if dreams could be trusted.

I dumped the tea into the sink and went and pulled a bottle of scotch from the pantry and splashed a hefty portion into a tumbler. It burned going down and brought tears to my eyes. I suppose the elves in Tír na nÓg would be offended at my traitorous choice of beverage, but frag them. I hadn't been on speaking terms with either Tir for quite some time.

But what to do about the dreams?

Perhaps the shamans in NAN would be willing to listen. But then I remembered the dustup we'd had before the Great Ghost Dance. They hadn't been too happy to hear my predictions about the magical fallout from all the blood they'd planned to spill.

Idiots. If only they'd listened. I suspected then that this would be the result. Like bees to honey, it would draw the creatures again. And we'd had no time to plan. To prepare. This time the monsters from the past would lay waste to the whole world.

Are you waiting for me?

Have you been waiting for me?

Does your flesh crave my caress?

Do you remember? Remember the centuries of pain and humiliation?

Do you know how I have missed you?

2

The sound of his voice echoed inside me.

I went to the thermostat and pushed it up. To hell with the regs about fuel waste, I thought. A century ago, Caimbeul had given me a Renoir. I liked to look at it when I felt like this. Afraid and lonely in the dark hours before dawn when the past spreads before me like a black spill of ink.

I flicked my hand and the illusionary wall I'd created long ago vanished. It was a simple enough spell, though in the past few centuries there'd been little enough magic to go around.

That was changing.

The last few years—a human life span—just a drop to me—had seen such a burst of magical energy and growth. The Awakening, they called it on their ugly little trids. Oh, I know Dunkelzahn found this brave new world far too fascinating, but he'd been dreaming for more than five thousand years. What would he know of it? He hadn't seen what the world had become.

I stepped into my room. The walls were windowless and covered in heavy oak paneling. Artwork and bookcases covered every available space, crammed full of everything I found precious. Centered on the north wall was the Renoir.

It was of a young woman and a little girl sitting on a balcony. The woman was wearing a brilliant red hat and she had a face of such sweetness that just looking at her almost hurt. I remembered when he'd painted it. A beautiful copy used to hang in the Chicago Art Institute, but I think it might have been destroyed during the riots in 2011.

So much beauty was lost then.

Here in my secret room I kept the relics of so many dead worlds. Of course dead worlds are all around us. They're just so much a part of our lives that we stop thinking about it. In London, five-hundred-year-old buildings snuggle next to glass columns built yesterday. Asphalt poured in nineteen-fifty is worn down by the wheels of a thousand rigs never dreamed of until five years ago. And the sweetmeats dance in nightclubs with rags on their backs sewn in sweatshops during the eighties. But that was just a momentary madness. A fad. A passing whimsy of fashion.

The things I'd distract myself with at times like that.

And here too were memories from a place and time out of mind. A place as unreal to this world as any trideo fantasy. What possessed me to recreate what I could remember? That time was done. Over. Dust.

Right.

Then why were there pictures painted by artists far greater than I, depicting places described by me? Why had I done it? Why had I asked Francisco Lucientes to recreate those nightmare visions? What madness had I unlocked from his mind? For surely he saw them—saw the demons.

His painting leaned against the wall, face down. I reached out and turned it around. Curators from every museum of the world would kill to have this lost treasure. Could they have understood it came not from Goya's demented vision, but from mine?

It showed a forest of such expanse that it fled from the viewer's sight back into a ghostly oblivion. Standing in the foreground were two people: a male and a female. She was human, slight of build with a curious face. He was an elf, tall and lithe with dark hair and a small goatee. Growing from his body were thorns.

The skin was puckered where the thorns protruded from his flesh. They ran across his face and showed as stark points across the back of his hands. A thousand slashes rent his tunic, letting the thorns escape.

I reached out and almost touched their faces with my fingertips.

Tears were streaming down my cheeks as hot and warm on my face as the blood that once fed that great forest. Blood poured from the wounds of my people.

But that wasn't the worst of what had been in that time.

My own complicity. Could such acts of evil ever be forgiven? Or forgotten?

I tried to push these dark thoughts away. But the dream wouldn't let me go. Wouldn't let me forget. I'd let myself become distracted by worldly matters. I'd forgotten why I was here.

I swallowed the last of the scotch. A pleasant heat had settled into my limbs. Perhaps now I would be able to sleep. With a simple gesture the illusionary wall was once more in place. I went upstairs. After closing the drapes, I settled under the quilts and comforters. But I couldn't bring myself to turn off the light. A childish notion, but it gave me some comfort.

And small comfort was all I would have for a long time to come.

A vast forest stretches out before her. Green and lush. Beautiful and deadly. And there are secrets. Terrible secrets. She steps forward and feels that she is sinking into something. Looking down, she sees her foot being swallowed by a pool of blood.

3

Dreams, I thought, *can't hurt you.*

The day was dreary and overcast. They usually were here. It was well past noon before I managed to pull myself from bed. Despite the scotch and leaving the light on, I didn't manage to sleep until after the sun rose.

Normally, I would have downloaded the morning *Times* and printed it out while I made tea. But I felt restless and penned-in by the house. I threw on jeans, boots, and heavy sweater, then grabbed my leather jacket as I went outside. It was late October and already the wind was blowing colder from the north.

It took me a few minutes to climb down to the beach. During the night it had rained and the path was muddy. I slipped a little as I ran down it. The sharp tang of the air cleared my mind.

Dreams, only dreams.

But I suspected they weren't. I'd had premonitions like this before. Before the Great Ghost Dance in 1888. And again before the one in 2014. Before the first VITAS plague. Before the start of goblinization in 2021. Each time I'd seen what was to come and I couldn't stop it.

Oh I'd tried, but the others weren't willing to listen. But they rarely thought about the consequences of anything that was happening. It has been that way for far too long. They've forgotten. Or didn't believe the danger was so close at hand.

I was so engrossed with my morbid thoughts that by the time I looked up, I'd gone onto my neighbor's property. He was a surly bastard and hated the fact that he had an elf for a neighbor. What was it he called me? Ah yes, a pointy-eared, pencil-necked, daisy-eating nigger. The last I assumed had to do with my skin color. It took every ounce of self-restraint I had not to slowly pull his tongue out his hoop the hard way.

But the Brits had an annoying habit of frowning upon murder. Especially when it involved a human and any sort of "meta" being. However, there were plenty of elves among the nobility in the UK, and I actually had good relationships with them. I hated to burn karma with them on someone who would be more annoyed by my continuing presence.

I turned and made my way back to the house. The fog had burned off finally and it was looking to be a rare sunny day. My security system let me back in with a cheery, "Good morning. It's October 20, 2056. The temperature is 9 Celsius outside . . ." It rambled on and on, and once again I reminded myself to have the thing removed. But I always forgot. So tomorrow it would be the same, "Good morning. It's October 21, 2056. The temperature is . . . blah blah blah."

As I pulled off my boots in the mud room, I found myself whistling an old tune. Well, maybe not whistling, more a tuneless wheeze.

Look on the bright side of life . . . dee, dah, dee dee deedilty dah.

I couldn't remember any more of the words. That used to drive Caimbeul crazy when we were together. My inability to remember more than a few snatches of lyrics from any song. Sometimes I even got the words wrong. What was that called? Oh, yes, mondegreens.

The kitchen was warm and I set the kettle on to boil on the flat heating element. I went upstairs and started the water for a bath. Stripping out of my clothes, I grabbed my robe and wrapped it around me. The kettle had begun to whistle and I went downstairs to fix tea.

In a few moments I had a tray all set to take upstairs. Sheer decadence to dispel the night fears. Tea and scones while taking a hot bath. Maybe later I'd read—from a real book with pages.

I'd just settled into the tub when the telecom beeped. Happens every time. As the machine picked up, I heard Caimbeul's voice.

"Aina, I know you're there," he said.

I gave a universal gesture for contempt and went back to drinking my tea. I hadn't heard word one from him in eight months. Frag him if he thought I was going to get out of a nice warm bath.

"Look," he said. "I'm en route to the UK. I should be landing in about an hour. Things have been happening. Things you need to know about. I have it all under control now, but we need to talk. I'll be up to Arran in about four hours."

I closed my eyes. The uneasiness that I'd almost dispelled was back. For Caimbeul to come here out of the blue meant something was up. Something big. The dreams came back to me. I shivered. The water had gone cold and I suddenly didn't like lying there naked and vulnerable.

Quickly, I finished washing my hair and got out of the tub. As I dressed, I tried not to dwell on Caimbeul's unexpected visit. Whatever the reason for it, I would know soon enough.

And I doubted the news would be good.

It is dark.

A blackness so thick and heavy it feels like a weight against her eyes. It is suffocating, this darkness. It feels as though she is being swallowed up by it. Being turned into it . . .

4

Caimbeul was late.

Though I wasn't surprised, I was annoyed. It wasn't as though I were looking forward to seeing him, but if you drop in on someone with "important" news, you'd bloody well better be on time.

I'd made tea with all the things Caimbeul liked. Scones, of course, with lemon curd. Those ridiculous little sandwiches with the crusts cut off, slices of cake, tarts. He had a sweet tooth. But now the sandwiches had gone hard and the cake was stale.

I'd switched from tea to sherry, then to scotch. And still no Caimbeul.

Finally, six hours after he'd said he'd arrive, I heard the crunch of tires across my gravel.

I waited until I saw him emerge alone from the car before opening the door. Even though I had security sensors, you can't be too cautious.

"Prompt as usual, I see," I said.

"Ah, Aina, still charming as ever," he replied. "No 'How are you? Why are you late?' You wound me."

I snorted.

"Please, spare me the usual dancing," I said. "It's cold out here. Come inside."

I turned and went into the house. Behind me I could hear him getting his bag and shutting the doors to the car.

"Lock the door and switch the system back on," I called over my shoulder.

He muttered something under his breath, but oddly enough he did as I asked. I went into the great room where I'd started a fire earlier that evening. Sometime between the sherry and the scotch.

"Did you leave that woman at home?" I asked.

"Yes," he said as he shrugged off his coat and tossed it on the couch. He flopped down into one of the wing chairs in front of the fire. I handed him a snifter of brandy and poured myself another scotch.

"I'm surprised. I'd've thought you'd bring her along to iron your shirts. Or something."

"Or something?" he asked. Coy, that one.

"Whatever it is you do with girls young enough to be your great-great-great-great-great-great-great-great-great-great-great-great-great-great-great-great-great-great-great—"

He held up his hands. "I get the picture."

"Oh, please, I don't want to hear about your peculiarities in that area."

"Do you care?" he asked. "What goes on between us is none of your business."

I turned away from him, stung by his remarks. Of course his life wasn't my concern. It hadn't been for centuries. But old habits die hard.

The silence stretched out between us. Once I enjoyed them. But now it felt awkward and tense. I longed for things to be as they once had, but it was far too late for that. As usual.

"I had a terrible time getting through UK customs," he said at last.

"Were you carrying anything?" I asked as I turned and walked toward him. He gestured for me to sit across from him as though this were his house and not mine.

"No."

"Made any enemies in the UK lately?"

He smiled then. I was glad he wasn't wearing his makeup. That awful mask he'd adopted out of some perverse sense of humor. Wicked Caimbeul.

We chatted then about meaningless things. Things to distract us from the free-floating tensions of a failed romance and too many years of history.

The fire had begun to die down and we were both a little muzzy.

"So," I said. But it came out more like "show." "Why all the mystery about your visit?"

Part of me, foolishly, hoped that his surprise had to do with the sudden realization that he'd been momentarily insane all those years ago when he'd left me.

"I beat them," he said, his voice dropping into a slightly drunken, conspiratorial tone. "You've been

26

saying that NAN would bring them back with all that blood magic. And you were right, Aina."

I felt a cold finger touch my heart. Suddenly the alcohol warmth fled and I was wide-awake sober.

"What are you saying?" I tried to keep my voice from shaking, but I failed. He didn't notice, though.

"They tried to get back, but I stopped them," he said. "Ah, well, I did have some help. A group of shadowrunners I enlisted. We went and played our little games on the metaplanes. God, it was fantastic. I haven't felt so alive since—I don't know when. Can you imagine it? Just my wits against them.

"Oh, there was some business with them recently in Maui, but that was easy enough to handle."

He gave a pleased laugh. Full and rich. I hadn't heard that tone in his voice in so long I'd almost forgotten he could sound that way. Had it been anything else to bring this joy about I would have been delighted, but all I wanted to do was shake him. Hard. Laughing and enjoying this . . . this catastrophe.

It was just like him to think he'd finished them off. What hubris. What ego.

" . . . And then I told them the story about Thayla," he was saying. "And I sent them on a quest to find her voice."

"Did it work?"

"Of course it did," he said, indignantly. "What do you take me for? A dilettante? I know we've had our disagreements, but even you can see what a feat this is."

"What I see is your ego is out of bounds again. In

your endless fascination with being involved in the machinations behind things, you've missed the point. As usual."

"You're jealous," he said.

"What?"

"You're jealous."

"Of what?" I was baffled at this sudden turn in the conversation.

"Of me. Of my power. You couldn't stand it when I surpassed your abilities."

"Don't be asinine."

"Oh, do you deny it?" he asked. He had a competitive, smirky expression on his face that I wanted to slap off.

"I won't even dignify that with an answer. The things which you pursue, Caimbeul, are vainglorious and, ultimately, irrelevant."

"That's something else you do," he said. "You always call me Caimbeul. I haven't been called by that name in three hundred years."

"Very well, Harlequin," I said. "But this is all beside the point. The point is you think the Horrors have returned and that you have beaten them single-handedly, don't you? Or at least once. I have no idea what actually happened in Maui because you always leave things out when it's not all about you."

He gave me an annoyed look.

"Very well, Aina," he said sullenly. "There was a group of kahunas using blood magic on Haleakala. They managed to open a portal—some of the Enemy even managed to get through. But they were stopped in time. They were sent back into the void.

"See, nothing to worry about."

"Let's see. First, you encounter them on the metaplanes. You manage to 'defeat' them there. Next, some of them manage to breach this plane. And you think they've been dealt with?

"Well, I've been having dreams lately and I think you're wrong. I think you failed."

He laughed.

"Aina has a dream and we're all supposed to tremble in our boots. Is that it?"

"I had forgotten this charming side to your personality, Caimbeul. I've been right before."

"And you've been wrong."

"Not often."

He didn't have an answer for that.

"I thought you would be thrilled at this news," he said at last. "You're the only one who still understands what it was like. Back then. During the Scourge."

I shrugged. "There's always Alachia," I said. "And Ehran. Oh, but I forgot about your tiff with him. Surely they remember."

"Alachia sees it differently than we do. She always has. And Ehran isn't worth a pimple on a troll's butt. As for the others—"

"Don't hold back, Caimbeul, how do you really feel?"

After giving me a nasty look, he went and refilled his glass.

"Bring me some water," I said.

In a moment, he placed a tumbler in my hand and settled himself opposite me again. Another long silence played out between us. The water was cool and washed the strong taste of the whiskey out of my mouth.

"Tell me what happened," I said at last. "The first time."

He didn't answer me for a moment. Then he spoke.

"They were constructing a bridge, of sorts, using the energy spike from the Ghost Dance as a locator. They are as foul as I remembered, Aina. No, perhaps worse, for it has been so long since I'd seen them that they'd begun to blur in my memory.

"I had to test the runners to be sure they had what it took to stand against the Enemy. For the most part they succeeded. One fell during the trials, but they accomplished what I set them to do. They retrieved the Voice, but didn't make it back to the bridge before a man named Darke captured me. The bastard was working with the Enemy and had been following me across the metaplanes the whole time. And I'd thought I was tracking him.

"He was performing blood magic to corrupt the site. How many children were sacrificed I'll never know. But Thayla sang and the enemy fell back, and now we're safe."

I almost choked on my water.

"Wait a minute," I said. "That all ties up a little too neatly. Thayla may be able to keep them at bay, but who will protect her from people like Darke?"

"Oh, some of the runners stayed with her," he said casually.

"But you didn't volunteer for that duty," I said.

"Don't be ridiculous," he said. "I'm far too valuable to be tied to one spot like that. Besides, as long as she's there, they can't get through."

"Not there, at any rate," I said. "And you're sure the creatures were driven back in Maui?"

"Of course," he said.

And how I wanted to believe him.

I stared into the fire. Long ago, according to our legends, Thayla's voice had driven the Horrors off. She had sacrificed herself for her people, like any great monarch would. Perhaps Caimbeul was right. Maybe he had accomplished it. Maybe he had driven them back. For now.

I relaxed a little. Maybe now there would be time to plan. To prepare. To warn those who needed to know.

The telecom beeped, startling me out of my thoughts.

"Who could be calling at this hour?" I wondered aloud.

"It might be for me," he said. "I left this number."

Oh, splendid, I thought. *Just what I need, Caimbeul's little friends with my restricted number.*

"Hello," I said into the old-fashioned videoless receiver I'd had installed in this room.

There was a long pause, then a loud burst of static. I jerked back, dropping the receiver onto the floor.

"Aina," I heard. The sound filled the room. An impossibility. And, oh sweet mother, I knew that voice.

31

"Aina," it said. "I have come back. I have come for you."

Then the line went dead.

"What was that?" Caimbeul demanded.

The room was cold. Colder than the dead of winter. Colder than the grave. For I knew from long experience that there were things worse than death.

"That," I said, my voice shaking, "was the past come back to haunt us, Harlequin. You didn't stop them from coming through on Maui, my dear. One of them is here. Now. And he's coming for me."

She is standing on a cliff overlooking the sea. The gulls dive for fish, crying with their broken voices. Below on the beach, a boy and girl play. They chase each other, leaving footprints in the sand that are washed away by the incoming tide.

The children's high-pitched voices float up to her, but she can't make out what they're saying. Then, as she watches, the sea turns red and bleeds onto the beach.

5

"Don't be ridiculous," Caimbeul said.

"Are you deaf?" I asked. "You were here. You heard it."

"A prank, perhaps," he said.

"That was no prank and you know it," I said. "I *know* that voice."

I turned away, running my hands over my arms to warm them. It had been so long. A time out of mind. Even so, I would never forget that sound. The sound of Ysrthgrathe's voice.

Like chalk on a blackboard. Like the whisper of a child. Like breaking glass. Like the dear departed. Whatever would be most effective.

A fine, cold sweat broke out on my back. *No, I*

thought, *I'll not give way to that so fast.* I clamped down on the panic. He'd be expecting that. No, I'd have to be careful and deliberate.

"It's only one," Caimbeul said. "We can deal with one."

"It's not just one," I said angrily. "Don't you remember anything I told you then about him? I seem to recall that we did spend some time talking all those years ago. Or is your memory as convenient as it ever was?"

"I thought we agreed not to discuss that time," he said. "But you keep bringing it up."

"I'm not discussing that time. I'm asking you if you remember what I told you then about Ysrthgrathe."

"That's a roundabout way of doing it."

"Will you shut up and listen? Frag it, you are so oblivious to everything but yourself. Didn't you hear a word I said then? Oh, I give up."

I spun about and strode from the room. I had to get to my grimoire. There were preparations to be made.

When the last of my defenses was in place, I began to relax a little. It concerned me that I might be making even more of a target of myself. Strong magic stuck out like a sore thumb these days. But it didn't really matter, he'd already found me.

Caimbeul knocked on the door to my study.

"Go away," I said.

"Don't be difficult, Aina," he said. "Let me in."

"No, no, dear Harlequin," I replied. "I don't wish to trouble you."

I heard him sigh. Loudly and dramatically so I would hear.

"Let me in," he said.

I walked over to the door and opened it.

"Oh, it's the great Harlequin come to pay a visit to the poor unenlightened masses. Oh, please show us your bountiful insight. We are honored by your presence. May we kiss your hem?"

"I was a bit . . . difficult," he began.

"No, you were an ass," I said.

"Very well, an ass. You always did get sarcastic when you were upset."

"How insightful of you," I said. "But you've got it a little wrong. I'm not upset. I'm scared. And if you had a bit of sense, you'd be frightened too."

He began to circle my study slowly, gently touching the books, totems, scrolls, and other bits of arcana I'd carefully catalogued. Some was only theory, some was practical. I knew he had an impressive accumulation of his own, but I also knew that I had been at this longer.

"What's this?" he asked, pulling a thick tome from a shelf.

"That," I said as I walked over and plucked it from his hand and stuck it back on its shelf, "is none of your concern. I'm certain you have five or six just like it at home."

An annoyed and interested expression crossed his face.

"I don't understand why you're so worried," he

said. "You've dealt with him in the past. As I recall, Vistrosh told me the most amazing story about how you vanquished him."

Rubbing my eyes with the heels of my hands, I sighed.

"Did he tell what really happened?" I asked. "Or was it turned into some of kind of ridiculous tale? Let me see if I can recount his version: 'And then Aina threw her arms wide to the skies and caused a blast of heavenly fire to consume the monster. The creature gave one last wail of angry despair and vanished into the void.' "

Caimbeul dropped into my heavy leather wingback chair and put his feet up on my desk.

"Yes," he said. "It was something like that."

"Well, you know as well as I that that's not exactly how these things happen. Oh, certainly I managed to overcome Ysrthgrathe, but it wasn't the simple matter Vistrosh would have had you believe. It almost killed me and I sacrificed more than you can possibly imagine."

"Like your grimoire?" he asked.

"Yes," I replied. "I unmade myself. You remember what I'd done. All those scars. The years and years of blood magic. Everything. I gave it all up to send him back. To imprison him. And now he's returned.

"Then I had so much power. Look at me now. What are you doing?"

He had picked up my grimoire and was leafing through it, making interested noises every few pages. I grabbed it from his hands, shocked at such a breach of etiquette.

"And I don't expect you to be any help," I said. "You're too damn selfish."

"The Enemy was stopped or we'd be dealing with more than one of them now. You're letting something that happened millennia ago affect you now."

"Don't tell me the past has no hold over you, Caimbeul. We both know what a lie that is."

"This is precisely the reason I left you," he snapped. "You pick and pick and pick."

"That's right," I said. "I'm no Sally, or Susan, or whatever-her-name-is-this-decade who fawns over you like you were some sort of demi-god. Doesn't fragging a sycophant lose its appeal after a while?"

He pushed himself up from the table in an angry rush.

"This bickering isn't getting us anywhere," he said. "What are you planning to do?"

Hugging my grimoire close to my body, I walked to the window and pulled back the drapes. It had begun to rain, and every so often the craggy land was lit by lightning. Bare country, wild and untamed.

"I've put up some protections, but I'm not sure how effective they'll be. I wish . . . Well, I might as well wish for the sun to rise in the west. What's that old adage? 'If wishes were horses, beggars would ride.' "

Caimbeul came up behind me. I could see him reflected in the window. A flash of lightning; the desolate land outside. The darkness; Caimbeul's image in the glass.

"I think you should tell the others," he said.

"Why don't you tell them? Your relations with them have always been better than mine."

"Because, Aina, I'm not convinced. You are. You will be more effective. Tell them."

"Tell them what?" I asked. "That I've had dreams and there has been one very strange telecom call?"

"Don't dodge it," he replied. "They'll have to listen to you. The ones who matter will know what it means."

I dropped the curtains and skirted around him. He was close enough that I could feel the warmth of his body.

"Why do you want me to do this?" I asked. "What have you got up your sleeve?"

He shrugged.

"I suppose your reaction has something to do with it," he said. "In all the time I've known you, I've never seen anything unnerve you so much as that call. Your hands are shaking even now. And when you heard that voice I thought you might faint. And, Aina, you're not the fainting type."

I smiled. I couldn't help it. He could still do that to me. Even in the worst moments, he had a knack for pulling it out of me.

"You're forgetting about Dunkelzahn and that ancient business," I said. "I doubt they're likely to have forgiven me for that."

"Probably not," he replied. "But you must try."

"And where do you suggest I try first?" I asked. "Tír na nÓg? Let's see ... I have such close relationships with the Elders there. Alachia in particular.

Yes, we've become the best of friends since that nasty business with the dragons. Oh, I'm sure she'll help my cause.

"And then there's Tir Tairngire. My relationship with Aithne is particularly strong. After Hebhel and Lily, I doubt he would piss on me were I on fire. Not that I blame him."

"That was a long time ago," he said. "There are more pressing issues than things and people dead and gone."

I made a slow circuit of my study. So many years of keeping track of the wisdom. Anticipating this time. Now that it was here, I was reluctant to act. No, afraid to act.

"Once, a long time ago, someone said to me that memory is all we have. Even as we speak, there is a slight lapse in time between what we hear and what we understand. All our experience is a kind of lag.

"Everything is memory, Caimbeul. Nothing has any meaning without it. 'He who cannot remember the past is condemned to repeat it.' See, even a human philosopher understood it. And he blinked out in a heartbeat.

"Don't kid yourself, Caimbeul. The past is very much with us."

I closed my eyes and let the past wash over me like the sea rushing over the shore.

Three birds are sitting on a branch. They are about to soar into the blue sky when an arrow pierces the hearts of two of them.

The third bird flies away, frightened and lonely. She knows the hunter is after her. Will always be after her.

6

We have always been a meddlesome race of beings, we Elders.

I suppose it comes from a long time of being privileged. Few have known of us. And none have been able to stop us from doing what we wanted. Oh, well, there was that business with the great worms, but even they must sleep eventually.

What was that amusing little saying from the comix? "Who Watches the Watchmen?" I used to see it scrawled across the bottoms of bridges and on the sides of buildings during the late nineteen-nineties.

So, though we'd been given a thrashing, while the cat's away (or the monstrous serpents), the mice will play. And so we did.

Myself, I have always preferred a low profile. None of the flash that has marked the passage of my fellows. The tales that have floated about me were easily written off as fables. That wasn't by accident, for I have believed for a long time that our presence is more a danger than a boon.

Perhaps had I been more vigilant, certain events of the past wouldn't have come to pass.

I had been traveling to England. Why, I can't remember now. Although I believe it had something to do with that collection of stones in Wiltshire. There were rumors of power there. Tremendous magical power. It was whispered in the harems and in council rooms. In market places and among the nomads. There were always places of power and this was one of them.

Stupidity.

That's how I came to be there. Had I bit of sense in my head I would have left them all to die. Hacking their lungs out, puking up what they'd barely managed to down a moment before.

Ignorant, superstitious peasants.

I knew there was a reason I'd stayed in the east for so long. In the east I wasn't looked upon as a black devil. The color of my skin was hardly commented upon.

But here among these backwards Englishmen with their pasty skin and bad teeth I was something to be feared, hated, and possibly killed. And the place they'd put me in might well do that.

It was called the Tower, but, of course, it wasn't. More like several castles and towers collected together. Not that I'd had much of a chance to see any of it. I'd been brought here in the middle of the night and hadn't seen much of the light of day since. Sometimes I wondered if anyone even remembered I was there.

Once a day a jailer slid a plate of bread and porridge through the grate. I could hear him muttering catechisms under his breath. It would do him little good and likely lose him his head, given the political mood. But don't we all fall back upon the icons from our youth? The stories we recite to keep the monsters at bay.

And that was how I knew I must appear. Oh, I'd lost the pointed ears, thank goodness. The more obvious signs of my elven condition were muted now. Magic was at a low ebb, though for some reason belief in it had never been higher. There were more charlatans and mountebanks claiming to turn lead into gold than you could swing a dead cat at. And they did a great bit of that, too. To drive out the demons.

Demons like me with my black skin and my white hair. My hair I could dye. Luckily, my eyes had changed to a brownish-gray color; otherwise I'd probably already be dead. *What would they make of Vistrosh and his ceathral skin and pink eyes?* I wondered.

But here I was locked up tighter than a miser's hoard.

And how had I come to be here? My own weaknesses, as usual.

"Help us," I'd heard.

I looked down and saw a young child, a girl, maybe eight. She wore a ragged tunic and her feet were bare and dirty. What desperation drove her to ask for help from any passing stranger? Much less one who looked like me.

"They're sick," she said.

"Who is sick?" I asked.

"Everyone," she replied. "Everyone except me."

But she didn't look well herself. Her eyes were bright and glassy and as I drew closer, I could feel the heat of fever radiating off her.

"Please," she said. Her hands reached out and I thought she might actually touch me, but she pulled away.

"What makes you think I could do any good?" I asked.

"Someone has to," she replied. "Or I'll be all alone. They'll . . . die."

I didn't want to help them. For as far back as I could remember I'd been trying to keep out of these things. To let Fate take her own course. It wasn't for me to decide. There were other matters that needed my attention. But as I looked into that pale feverish face another child came to my mind, and I found myself being led into the rude thatched hut.

The air was thick with the odor of a low-burning peat fire. There was a hole cut in the roof to let the smoke escape, but that only helped a little. Pallets lined the edge of the room. On them lay several people, all of whom were in various stages of the same sickness.

The grippe.

Why these people were so ill from it I didn't know. It was a common enough problem—not as frightening as the plague or cholera, which could pass through a town and leave it devastated in a matter of days or weeks.

At my feet lay an elderly woman. I knelt down beside her and took her wrist in my hand. Under my fingers her pulse felt erratic. I was closer to the power here; the pull of it too tempting to resist. As my eyes closed I began to see the pattern of her life. Thin and threadbare. Bleak colors woven together with an odd shock of bright blue.

It was so difficult to hold on to what I was seeing. The images were blurred and hazy, slipping away from me if I hesitated for a moment. But, healing her would be simple enough, I saw suddenly. It had been so long since I'd taken the risk. Since I'd wanted to.

There was a faint sound. It broke my concentration and I turned toward it. There, shadowed in the doorway, stood the girl. For a moment her image blurred with one from my memory. I knew then I would help them, regardless of the risk.

Again, I took the woman's wrist. Tapping into what little reserves I'd tucked away, I focused all my concentration into bringing back the weave of her life. The heat flew through me then, sliding into her body, burning out her fever and pain. Hot ribbons of health wove themselves into her body.

I released her wrist then, exhausted by this minor act. I smiled a bit at this, I who had brought armies to their knees with a flick of my wrist, swooning at this child's play.

And what did my generosity get me?

A private room in the bloody Tower.

The people I helped weren't to blame. They couldn't have been expected to keep quiet about their miraculous healings, I suppose. Though I suspect the tale was embellished by the time it reached the ears of the clergy.

The Protestants and the Catholics had been going at it ever since Mary came to the throne, but the one thing they agreed on was that anything smacking of witchcraft was to be dealt with severely.

For some reason the local priest, who was the first person to see me after I was captured, didn't want to kill me right off. Perhaps it was my skin, or maybe he hoped to gain points with bishop. At any rate, I was taken to London and then sent to the Tower.

Where I remained for months.

I'd heard that there were prisoners here who'd been forgotten for years. But I tried not to dwell on that.

Spring passed, then summer.

All Hallows Eve.

Dark came early. Through my slit of a window, I could see the fine mist ushering a heavy fog. The flickering torches looked unreal and ghostly. A perfect night for the devil's work. If you believed in that sort of thing.

I'd been sitting in the dark for several hours. The worst thing about imprisonment was boredom. But this wasn't the first time I'd been in such a situation. Then I heard it. A faint sound from down in the base of the tower.

Then footsteps on the stone steps. They were

coming to kill me, I knew it. After all this time, they had remembered and were dispatching me at last. The least I could do was go to my death on my feet. But somehow I couldn't force myself to move from the cold stone floor where I sat.

The sound of voices. I thought they might be arguing. Then more footsteps. The lock was opened and the door swung in.

I put my hand up against the sudden brightness of a lamp. A rustle of fabric. Any moment now I would feel the burn of the blade.

"You may leave us now," a voice said.

A voice I knew.

I dropped my hand and blinked. It couldn't be, yet it was.

Standing across from me, robed in heavy velvet and fur, was Alachia.

"What are you doing here?" I asked.

She frowned. "You never have learned any manners," she said. "Do you not know that you are to rise in the presence of a queen?"

I snorted. "Blood Wood is long gone," I said. "Its ashes have been forgotten more times than either of us can remember. You're no more a queen than I."

"You never were ambitious," she said.

"No, just not foolish and vain."

Her frown deepened. Even with such a withering expression on her face, she was still beautiful. The skin was as pale, the hair as fiery red, and the eyes as blue. Not as stunning as she'd been, but part of that was due to the changes in the magic. Now her beauty was more human.

"You are an annoyance," she said. "But you are my cross to bear. Isn't that an amusing expression? Tell me, aren't you curious as to why I am visiting you?"

I didn't answer. I knew it would annoy her. How odd that even after all this time we fell back into our old patterns.

"Well, I'll tell you," she said. Her voice was gleeful and fairly danced with excitement. "In a fortnight, I am again to gain a throne. Admittedly, not as impressive as those I've left behind me, but it will do in the meantime."

"What are you talking about?" I asked.

"Haven't you heard?" she asked. "Mary is dying and Elizabeth is to be crowned queen. Don't you think Henry is turning over in his grave? Killing off that poor girl's mother because she couldn't give him sons. Brutal bastard."

"What has that to do with you?"

"Why, my dear, haven't you guessed yet?"

I stared at her for a moment, then, through the dullness of my mind, comprehension.

"Are you mad?" I asked.

"What do you mean?" she said coyly.

I was staggered. She'd been interfering for years in things that weren't our business—but this—this was too much.

"How do you propose to achieve this miracle?" I asked. "Don't you think people will see the difference between you?"

"Ah, I have been planning this for years," she said. "It has taken an immense amount of time and energy. Do you think that I just popped up yesterday? Oh no, I have been Elizabeth for quite some time."

"But her servants, teachers, surely someone . . ."

"A simple enough matter to arrange. A spell here, a spell there . . . and patience. Such patience as you have never known. And now, at last, I'm in a position where I can do something."

I could only stare at her. It was madness—sheer and utter madness. How she could possibly think she could maintain such a farce was beyond me.

"Aina," she said, "you have always been so short-sighted. We can control what happens over the next thousand years. Make the world over in our image. Think of it—the power will come back again. Not this trickle, but a deluge of energy to rip loose the moorings of the world—unless we make certain of the proper order of things. Humans are sheep. We will always rule them.

"The legends and tales you strew about aren't enough. We must have more. We must control them. This is our destiny."

Even had I wanted to stand, I didn't think my legs would hold me. What she was proposing was monstrous. It went against everything I believed about our place. Our purpose. We had a duty to perform. We were to keep the world safe so that the knowledge would survive from age to age.

She knew what I did—how could she discard it all for so clumsy a form of power? But then, power had always entranced her. And so much of her mind would never be known to me. She was far older than I.

And I have lived so long that Sisyphus's chore looked like a blessing to me.

"You pervert what we are," I said.

"This pious attitude is quite boring, Aina," she said. "I think I liked you better before you lost your faithful companion. He certainly would never have tolerated such an attitude. And he could goad you into so many things."

I felt the blood draining from my face and blessed my dark skin. Cruelty was her hallmark. How could I have let my guard down for even a second? The energy drained from me then. I didn't have the strength now to battle with her.

"What has all this to do with me?" I asked.

She walked closer to me. The wide span of her skirts just touched the ragged hem of my cloak.

"I want your assurance that you won't interfere with my plans," she said. "I know you could make things difficult for me and I won't have it. There has been too much time and energy devoted to this for you to create problems."

"How did you know I was in England?" I asked.

"That was a happy accident," she said. "For the last few years I've made it my business to keep abreast of any rumors of witchcraft. When I heard about a dark-skinned woman with white hair who'd been arrested for sorcery, well, I assumed it must be you."

"Have you known all along that I've been here?" I asked.

"Of course," she said. "I just couldn't take any

action on it for a while. Besides, I wanted you out of the way until I decided what to do with you."

I closed my eyes. Knowing Alachia, she could keep me here for decades before letting me go. By that time I might well have lost my mind.

"What do you propose?" I asked.

"Just what I said. You keep out of my way in this matter. I will act as queen to this tiny nation."

"This is madness, Alachia," I said. "Why would you want this?"

"Because I need to rule," she said.

"And if I don't agree?"

"I'll find someplace where I can leave you to rot," she said. "You won't die, unfortunately. But you'll certainly wish you had. That is, if you still have your sanity intact after all those years locked up and alone. It's really not much of a choice, is it?"

She had me there. I couldn't stop her from what she was about. But I could certainly see my way clear to making her life difficult once she let me out.

"Very well," I said. "I agree."

She came to the throne on November 17, 1558 and ruled for an astonishing forty-five years. And at every turn I made her way as difficult as possible. Oh I didn't act directly; that has never been my way. But I knew people on both sides, and it was a simple matter to sow the seeds of distrust and paranoia. All I had to do was stir the pot. Between juggling the French and Spanish, she was forced to look to the welfare of the country.

Besides, it was a source of constant amusement to me that she was referred to as the Virgin Queen.

That wasn't the first, nor would it be the last, time she did such a thing. But the brazenness with which she acted in this matter always amazed me. And after that time, I always made sure to stop her whenever I could.

Do you think you'll escape me through the past?
Do you think that by telling them you'll be safe?
Don't you know that I've been waiting—
as patient as time itself?
Don't you know you can never stop me?

7

"I tried to stop her," I said.

"What?" asked Caimbeul.

I hadn't realized I'd spoken aloud.

"Nothing," I said. With a quick snap of my wrist I pulled the drapes together and shut out the storm. "I suppose I should pack."

There was the creak of leather as he settled back into my chair.

"So," he said, "you're going to tell them. Where will you go first?"

"The Seelie Court," I said. "It should be the least hostile reception."

"If you can find them."

This made me laugh.

"Ah, Caimbeul," I said. "That will be the easy part."

It was drizzling the next morning as we loaded our bags into Caimbeul's rental car. I'd set the alarm and cast spells, and as I locked the front door I had the terrible feeling that this would be the last time I would ever see Arran.

Damn them all, I thought. *If they would only have listened. If they'd stopped playing with things they only barely understood. Then I wouldn't have to leave my house and venture into matters I've spent hundreds of years avoiding.*

But I knew the worst of the bunch were the ones who knew the dangers and went ahead with their foolishness anyway. Damn them, too.

Caimbeul had opened the passenger-side door and stood there waiting for me to get in. I dropped into the synthleather seat, sniffing the vinyl scent of new car as I did. After shutting the door behind me, Caimbeul came around the front of the car and got in on his side.

"I made some plane reservations while you were still asleep," he said. "It was bloody expensive and I expect to be reimbursed."

"I can't believe you're bringing up money at a time like this," I said.

Out the corner of my eye I saw him shrug.

"I know you're good for it," he said.

"So are you. You've got piles of the stuff hidden everywhere. What's a plane ticket to you?"

"That's not it," he said, primly. "It's the principle of the thing."

"The principle of the ..." And then I couldn't continue because I was laughing too hard.

I contented myself with watching the passing scenery and playing with the vid, trying to get some decent signal to come in. But all I found were walls of noise and static. Finally I managed to tune in a prehistoric station that was doing a retrospective of turn-of-the-century music. Snapping off the trideo portion, I let the sounds wash over me. I confess I liked the older flat-screen stuff: Nine Inch Nails, Cold Bodies, Sister Girl's Straight Jacket. Nothing like a little atonality with my angst.

Every so often I would glance over at Caimbeul. Excuse me, Harlequin. I don't think that name will ever come trippingly to my lips. And I hate what it represents even more.

Yes, I know you think you understand him. You might even think you know him well, but you don't. I've known him for longer than either of us cares to remember. And he wasn't as you see him now. That stupid painted face. Though he wasn't what many would call handsome, I have always found him attractive. Maybe even beautiful. Oh, I know that sounds peculiar, but there is an aspect of ugliness that is so shocking and strange it becomes beauty.

And his wild hair, all gold and brown woven together. He'd let it grow long again, which I like. But he insisted on pulling it back in that ridiculous pony tail. It made me want to sneak up behind him with a scissors and cut it off. Either you wear it long or you don't was my way of thinking.

His hands lay easily on the wheel. I knew they were smooth and feminine with calluses on the fingertips. There was a hint of yellow between the first and second fingers where he held those Gaullets he smoked. And he smelled of tobacco and clean linen.

And I wondered whether he remembered those sorts of things about me. The little details that only come from intimacy.

"Will you turn that off?" he asked.

"I like it," I replied as I leaned forward and nudged the volume button up a little.

"I know," he said. "You always did have terrible taste in music."

"No, I've always had broad taste in music. Unlike you who only seem to like classical music and the occasional jazz group."

"I prefer to think of it as a refined taste."

"I know you do."

We didn't say anything else and I went back to watching the kilometers slip by as the rain streamed across the windows.

Edinburgh was crowded. Old ladies were crying and hugging uncomfortable-looking teens. Suits hurried by, oblivious to everything but their own sense of self-importance. I've never been too fond of corporate thinking. That whole bigger is better drek was what had led to most of the problems in the world, as far as I could tell. Okay, indoor plumbing was the one exception to this rule, but otherwise . . .

We found the gate for the flight to Tír na nÓg. As we came around the corner, I saw that the usual security measures were in place. All our luggage was going to be searched. There would be the usual weapons scan and the endless procession of bureaucratic red tape. Like I said: corporate thinking.

The worst of it was that once we got to the Tír, all this would begin again.

As we approached the head of the line, the elven official looked up from the display screen where he was sliding credsticks to check documentation. He gestured us forward, ignoring several people ahead of us.

"May I see your passports and visas?" he said. He tried to keep it polite, but you could tell he wasn't going to take no for an answer.

We handed over our sticks with our IDs and travel permits on them, and he asked us to step into a small room off the main corridor. As the door shut behind us I could hear the other passengers whispering to each other. You could cut the paranoia with a knife.

"Is there a problem?" Caimbeul asked.

The security drone didn't answer as he sat down at a display on the far side of a small formica table in the center of the room. The walls were a dirty white and one of the fluorescent lights flickered on and off erratically. I read his name off his badge: Clovis Blackeye. No wonder he was an officious prig. With a name like that I'd be a drekhead, too.

He was gaunt and stoop-shouldered for an elf. His hair was tied back into a ponytail and was shot through with premature gray. A perpetual expression of misery lined his face and made his eyes look sunken and bruised. He knew he would never be anything more than a low-level bureaucrat.

Sometimes there was no explaining UGE.

"I said, 'Is there a problem?' "

Clovis finally looked up from the screen. His beady eyes swung from Caimbeul to me.

"It says here that you're visiting relatives in Tír na nÓg. But it doesn't list who those relatives might be."

"Is that necessary?" I asked.

"How do we know you really have relatives in the Tír? Maybe you're from that other place, come to cause trouble."

"That other place?"

"Tir Tairngire. The fallen ones."

I glanced at Caimbeul and he rolled his eyes. Nothing worse than a *patriotic* officious prick.

"And perhaps we have relatives who don't want every low-level clerk knowing who *their* relatives are," I said.

His flat piggy nose flared slightly.

"That's not for you to decide," he said. "Now tell me or you don't get on that plane."

I leaned forward across the table then and grabbed his collar. For a moment I thought he might resist, but the force of my will kept him from moving. It was as easy as a snake hypnotizing a rat.

"Listen to me, little brother," I said in Éireann sperethiel. My accent might have been a bit off, but otherwise I was letter perfect. *"You are playing in things far beyond your knowledge or concern. You wish to know who we are to visit? Then come closer and I shall tell you."*

I jerked him across the table and whispered a name in his ear. The blood fled from his already pasty cheeks. As he pulled away, I let him see me—

57

really see me. These are the kinds of tricks I hate—
obvious displays of power—but he'd slotted me off.

"Now you can well imagine how annoyed this
person would be if they discovered their name came
up in this sort of situation," I said. "So I would suggest that we all forget this unfortunate incident."

Old Clovis was only too happy to oblige. He gave
us back our papers like he'd just discovered they'd
been tainted with VITAS. We were ushered onto the
plane without further delay. I settled into the thick
leather upholstered seats of the first-class section
and smiled at the attendant who handed me a glass
of single malt scotch.

"Was that really necessary?" asked Caimbeul after
she moved away.

"What?" I said, letting my eyes go wide and innocent.

"That show you put on back there."

The plane gave a little lurch as it backed from the
gate. I glanced out the scratched window. Below me
I could see the orange lights on the ground.

"No," I said. "We could have missed the flight
snaking around with him. But I didn't have the patience for it. Besides, he's going to be too scared to
tell anyone. He believes in the omnipotence of the
Elders. You could see it in his eyes."

"But you showed him . . ."

"I showed him what would impress him the most.
Some people are so literal."

"I missed you."

"What?" It was a strange and unexpected non-
sequitur. And I couldn't believe my ears.

"Well, I didn't miss the arguing. But I missed you when you get like this."

I didn't say anything to that.

It wouldn't have made any difference anyway.

She's running.

The forest is alive with sounds and smells. In the distance, the dying rabbit cries sound like a child's screams. The heavy scent of new-dug earth hangs in the air. Branches slap against her face, and no matter how she tries to push them away, they keep coming back.

Something is behind her. She doesn't know what it is—only that it will kill her if it can. Looking over her shoulder, she tries to see what it is. So she doesn't see when she steps off into space.

She's falling now.

Falling with nothing to save her.

8

I jerked awake as the plane passed into the Veil. It was a nasty jolt of reality, being sound asleep one moment and wide-awake the next. A tingling started at the nape of my neck and worked its way up my skull.

Pushing the plastic shade up, I peered out the window. There was nothing but thick gray and white clouds like the smoke of burning leaves. I struggled against the effects of the Veil. The clouds tried to form themselves into shapes. What part of my subconscious was being dredged up? I didn't want to know and pulled the shade down with a snap. We'd be on the ground in half an hour. I could hold out against the effects until then.

"Pretty potent stuff," said Caimbeul. "The Veil. It makes me wish they would use some other sort of protection."

I shoved a hand through my hair. It was virtually gone now. After centuries of having it long, I'd finally cut it all off. All that was left were spiky white sprouts about an inch and a half long. My head felt smooth and cool under my fingers.

"Too potent," I said. "They're only aggravating things."

"You've said that every time anyone's used magic on any scale."

I didn't answer him, knowing that we'd just run over the same ground again. The engines whined and I felt the thump as the landing gear lowered. Then I shoved the shade up again. We broke through the clouds and I could see buildings below us. From here everything looked small and not at all real. Up here we were still safe.

I closed my eyes then, breathing slowly and deeply to relax myself. I had my usual landing death-grip on the chair arms. Blowing up in a ball of fire was not the way I wanted to end my unnatural life. My ears popped several times and I opened and closed my mouth to help. Then I felt it.

The smooth calluses and the suede glide of Caimbeul's hand closing over mine. I didn't pull away. It was too comforting and familiar. I kept my eyes closed, not wanting to see when we burst into a huge ball of fire.

There was a sudden bounce and we were on the ground. Caimbeul's hand disappeared and I was left with only the memory of his warm touch.

Once, years ago, I lived in the United States.

I'd come to America during the eighteen-hundreds when news that the Sioux were using ritual magic drifted across the Atlantic to the fashionable parlors I frequented then. It was a topic of much conversation for a few months, until other, more interesting scandals pushed their way into idle gossip.

But I knew the Sioux were playing with dangerous mojo.

The reports told of self-mutilation to help the magic. Blood magic. It was too early for that sort of thing—unless they'd found a place of power. They were playing with forces they couldn't understand and wouldn't be able to control, even if by some freak chance they did work.

I booked passage on the next available steamer and was making my way west in a matter of weeks. There was no time for me to admire the rawness of the country. Everything was new here. Fresh starts for anyone willing to take it. The weight of history had barely settled onto the land.

But that is another part of the story. The time I am thinking of came later, in the late nineteen-thirties and early forties. I was living in Texas then. The war known as the War to End All Wars was barely cold. The embers of it still smoldered in the battlefields of

Europe. But apparently they weren't ready for them to be out yet. That little Austrian man stirred it all up again and the depths of his hateful vision wouldn't be known for another six years. But by then, it would be too late for us all.

But in Austin we didn't know about any of that. The world came to us through newspapers, magazines, radio—and through the movies.

It was a blistering hot summer. But that was nothing unusual. Most people left the city for cooler parts of the Hill Country. The ones who remained made do with fans, ice blocks, and shade. In the evening the temperature would drop into the high seventies. It was almost bearable.

Once the initial shock of the war wore off, life went on as usual. For the most part. Most Americans thought they would be exempt from the conflict. After all, what did it have to do with them, this bloody war in Europe?

And so, on this summer night with the heavy scent of lantana and moonflowers in the air, I went to the movies. Some people were afraid of being in closed places because of the polio, but that was never a concern of mine.

The theater was dimly lit and I used a fan given away at the local Herbert E. Butts grocery store to push the sweltering air about. The lights went down and the newsreel began. Of course, the war in Europe was the first item. I watched as scene after scene of destruction flashed across the screen. Many things were being blown up in Poland and France and England.

Then we were looking at images of happily waving crowds. The little man rode through them making his straight-arm salute to the frantically waving masses.

And then I saw her.

At first I couldn't believe my eyes, but the shot held and I knew what I was seeing was true. It was Alachia.

She was sitting in one of the cars in the rear of the procession. An expression of perfect happiness was etched in her face. A blond man with his hair slicked back and perfect Aryan features waved at the crowds while his other arm encircled her waist. He smiled down at her and she smiled back. They were gone in an instant, replaced by the image of refugees fleeing down some unknown road.

The screen went black and then the Parade of Fashions appeared. Sweat rolled down my face but I was suddenly cold. So very cold.

We rode the shuttle bus headed south toward Dublin, hooking up to Dorsett Street once we were in the city proper.

We'd made it through customs relatively easily. There was no need to resort to the sort of tactics I'd used on that idiotic bureaucrat from before. Like many of the Dublin streets, this one turned and bent and changed names. We took a left onto Church Street and headed south toward the river. Four Courts was to our left. The dome of the central building was covered in the green patina that comes to all copper as it ages. It was a beautiful piece of neoclassical work. All white columns and statuary at every corner. The fact that it was standing after all this time gave me a fleeting feeling of permanence.

As we crossed Whitworth Bridge, I looked out the window. Below us the Liffey River flowed a gray-jade color, the dark clouds of the late-October sky barely reflected in its depths.

At the next stop, we left the tram and cut across West High Street. It was a strange experience, to see almost as many elves as humans walking about. No one gave us a second look. Oh well, perhaps one or two. We were dressed better than the average Dub-liner. I know the reports out of the Tír have it that the land is green and milk and honey flow from every stream, but after all, this is Eire.

Poverty has been at the throat of the people for generations. And goblinization hadn't changed that. Perhaps no one was starving, but all was not well in the Tír.

At St. Nicholas Street we headed south and cut west before we reached St. Patrick's Park. I glanced back to see if anyone was following us. An old woman pulled a shopping cart filled with vegetables, but as far as I could see there was no one tailing us.

"How long since you've been here?" I asked Caimbeul.

"Oh, I get about," he said, shrugging.

"Meaning you've been here recently."

He gave me hard stare. "Yes. I was here recently. I was invited to attend a wedding."

"Whose wedding?"

"I'd rather not say."

"Because I wasn't invited?"

"Well, yes."

"Well, I don't care about that," I lied. Weddings were highly symbolic events in the elven community. Full of alliances and power-jockeying. Not being invited meant I wasn't considered a power anymore. That would hurt me when I went to the Court. No doubt Alachia's hand at work once more.

We worked our way across the maze of streets that led to St. Stephen's Green. Nestled next to ancient stone buildings were brick flats put up in the nineteen-hundreds next to chip-implanting shops. Dublin wasn't a flash city like New York or LA. She crept up on you and worked her charms in subtler ways. A hint of the past here. A bit of the future there.

Once we were in St. Stephen's I relaxed a little. I was certain no one was tailing us: the old woman had turned off on Bride Street. Since then, the crowd thickened and thinned, but no one seemed at all interested in Caimbeul and me.

"Where do you want to stay?" Caimbeul asked.

"Stephen's Hall?"

"Do they have a decent security rating?"

"Good enough," I said. "It's not like we're going underground."

The hotel overlooked St. Stephen's Green with its emerald grass and drooping willows. We checked in and followed the troll bell boy up to our suite.

We left a wake-up call for six.

* * *

The rains came at four. I woke to a crash of thunder and the sound of hail hitting the windows. For a moment I was disoriented and thought I was back in the kaer. A suffocating darkness pressed against me. But then I saw the night sky as Caimbeul opened the drapes.

"Where did this come from?" he wondered aloud.

"If I were more superstitious," I said, "I would say it was a sign."

"A sign?"

"Yes. They know we're here. But it's more likely this is the *Doineann Draoidheil.*"

He didn't say anything to that. Knowing he was watching there at the window made me feel safe. And as I drifted back to sleep, I smiled.

Tonight she doesn't dream.

9

Bells.

I swam up from the murky depths and realized before I opened my eyes that it was the telephone. *Couldn't they afford to replace these fraggin' antiques?* I thought. Swatting at the phone, I managed to drag it from its cradle and sent the base crashing to the floor. Damn things, I never got used to them when they appeared and now that they were obsolete, I was still plagued with them.

"Whazzit?"

"Your wake-up call." The voice was computerized and preternaturally perky. I hate that.

I let the receiver drop. It missed the base and thudded on the carpet. Burrowing further into the covers, I let the lovely blackness drag me down again.

"Aina," said Caimbeul, pulling the covers off me. "Time to get up."

I lay there for a moment not moving. It occurred to me that though we Elders weren't supposed to mortally wound one another, there was always a first time for everything. Instead, I rolled onto my back and glared at him in what I hoped would be a frightening manner.

"That won't work," he said. He was dressed in black. His hair was pulled back into that annoying ponytail. At least he'd laid off dyeing it red for a while. "I'm not even a little intimidated by your bad moods. I lived with them for years. They just don't impress me anymore."

I muttered something unintelligible, hoping it would be taken for a scathing remark. But it wasn't. He knew me too well.

Stumbling to the bathroom, I hoped that there was at least hot water for a shower.

We rented a car and made our way west from Dublin out of Dublin County through Kildare to Offaly and into Galway. A heavy mist lay over the land making the greens muted and soft. Much of the land had gone wild. I knew this was part of the Awakening.

The land was going back to what it was before humans had put their mark upon it. Remnants of that earlier time existed before the Awakening. The Giant's Causeway in Antrim was one such place. Some said it was cooling lava that produced the hexagon-shaped stones leading from the mountains down to the sea, but I knew better.

"How are you going to find the Court?" Caimbeul asked. "They could be anywhere."

"Yes, but those who know where they are keep to certain places. We're going there."

"To the tombs?"

"Yes, and other places."

"You know how I hate the tombs."

"Life is suffering, Caimbeul. Didn't you know that?"

Because of the fog, it took us four hours to reach The Burren. The land here was wilder than other areas of the Tír. Perhaps because the people who lived in this part of Ireland had never been far from their Celtic roots. Even before the Awakening, Gaelic was the primary language for large sections of Galway.

As we passed, I saw fingers of gray rock clawing up through the thin soil. Dark green thorn trees twisted against the fierce ocean wind. Sheer cliffs dropped down to rocky seashores.

The Burren was a flat plain of gray limestone rock. Deep fissures cut down into the slabs of stone, scarring the rock. The only things that grew there were wildflowers that sprang up between the cracks.

I parked the car and we started up the Burren. Once there would have been tourists clambering over the outcroppings. Now there was a stillness that hung in the air and seeped slowly into my bones.

"Come on," I said softly.

We made our way, for once not bickering about how fast or slow one or the other was going. I stopped every so often to pluck flowers that grew from the crevices. I wove them into necklaces as we walked. I kept one for myself and handed one to Caimbeul. He gave me a skeptical look, but slipped his into his pocket.

The mist was getting thicker and thicker as we walked. I stumbled over the uneven rock and wished I'd thought to bring a walking stick. Then we were upon it. A large fissure in the rock. It was large enough for one of us to slip through at a time.

"Well," I said. "I'm going down. You can wait here for me if you want."

Caimbeul gave a disgusted snort.

"You think they'll listen to you without me?" he asked.

I looked up at him then, deep into his forest-green eyes. We knew each other well, Caimbeul and I, and I knew this ploy for what it was.

"Oh yes, dear Harlequin," I replied. "I think they will listen to me very well. They know who I am."

It was cool in the cave. We were crawling on our stomachs down a long passageway with only a small light to lead us. I'd cast the spell once we'd found ourselves in this narrowing corridor and I couldn't hold my flashlight any longer.

"Remind me to tell you how much I enjoy crawling through a cave in my very best shoes and coat," Harlequin said.

"Don't complain," I replied. "It could be worse."

"How so?"

He ran into my heels and gave a little oomph.

"It could be wet."

"Oh, what a lovely thought."

Just then I crawled around a corner and popped out into a large cavern. Stalactites and stalagmites grew down from the ceiling and up from the floor.

In the center of the cavern was a lake. Its surface was mirror perfect and black as night.

I turned around and helped Caimbeul as he too crawled out. There was dirt and dust covering his clothes. He slapped at it, but it didn't help. When he looked up at me again, I could see the annoyance in his face. I put my finger to my mouth, then pointed at the lake.

I walked away from him toward the edge of the water. The only sound was the crunch of stones under my boots. As I reached the edge of the lake, I leaned over and picked up a small stone. Straightening, I spoke,

"Hear me, Fin Bheara, King of the Daoine Sidhe, King of the Dead. It is Aina. I would speak with you."

My voice rang out and echoed against the silent rocks. For a long moment there was nothing. No answering sound. Then, there was a grinding noise. The ground trembled and I stumbled a bit before regaining my balance.

The water began to bubble and boil. Steam rose from the surface and soon blanketed the entire room. From the water rose a boat. It was made of wood and gold. A throne was affixed in the center of the deck. Sitting in it was the spirit who liked to be known as Finvarra.

He was as I remembered, perhaps even larger than before. The power of the Awakening had seeped into his veins as well as mine.

The boat moved toward the shore where I stood, cutting smoothly through the water, leaving only the slightest wake to mar the perfect sheen. I could see no oarsmen or sails, but that is the way of faerie. It stopped about a meter from shore and rested there.

"Greetings, Finvarra," I said. "You do me a great honor."

He laughed. It was harsh and grating, and yet it sounded like music to me.

"Aina," he said. "Sweet mother. How may I help?"

"I would find the Seelie Court, Finvarra," I replied. "Though to hear some tell it, I am no longer considered a power in Tír na nÓg."

"Come down from there, Caimbeul," Finvarra said. "You make me nervous lurking about."

I heard Caimbeul curse as he slipped and slid his way toward us.

"You haven't answered my question," I said. "Where is the Seelie Court?"

Finvarra leaned back on his throne and studied me. I returned the favor. His gray eyes were as piercing as ever and the sharp planes of his face were more cruel than kind. A thin gold circlet rested on his brow. Long thin hands rested on bony knees. His clothing, made of leaves and bark and animal pelts, reminded me of what we'd worn in Blood Wood all those centuries ago.

Then I noticed that lying at his feet was a young woman. She was dressed in a tight purple dress with thigh-high black patent leather boots. Part of her head was shaved so the datajack she'd had implanted could be easily accessed. She seemed to be asleep.

"Up to your old tricks again," I said.

" 'Tis nothing," he said. "A harmless amusement."

"What would Oonagh say?" I knew I had to play along.

"What she doesn't know ... Besides, this is all rather off the point. You wish to know where the Seelie Court is currently residing."

"Yes."

"Perhaps they don't wish to be found."

"No. I suspect they don't. And I suspect I know why they don't want to hear from me."

Finvarra smiled at me. His teeth were yellow and very long.

"Now we're getting somewhere," he said. "Perhaps I can help you. If you are willing to do something for me."

"And what might that be?" I asked.

"A test," he replied. "A simple challenge of your will. My subjects will be more than happy to administer it. If you succeed, we take you to the Court. If you fail, well, that will be your lookout, won't it?"

"And who decides whether I win or lose?"

"Why that, dear mother, you will have to figure out for yourself."

With that, the boat sped away from me. It left barely a ripple in the water and the mist closed around it, hiding it from my sight. I stepped forward, the edge of the lake touching my toes. *What now?* I wondered.

"Well, that was helpful," said Caimbeul.

I spun about, ready to give him a cutting remark

when behind me something burst forth from the water and grabbed me.

In a flash I was being pulled down into the blackness. The water was freezing and I hadn't caught a breath. I fought against the urge to inhale. My eyes were open, but I couldn't see much. I looked down and saw that I was being held by a each-uisge. My legs were helplessly stuck to its chest and forelegs. Its clawed hands were clasped about my thighs. The head was that of a horse with razor-sharp teeth.

It would pull me down into the water until I drowned and then feast upon my flesh, except for my liver, which it would no doubt spit up at Caimbeul's feet. It was a prospect I didn't relish.

I let myself go limp, playing dead, hoping this would slow its descent. It did. Then I jerked my arms apart and uttered the words. Between my hands a whirling of water started. It began to glow and lit the each-uisge with blue light. The water spun faster and faster until it narrowed into a fine, laser-like point. I pointed it downward at the each-uisge's head. There was the muffled sound of a shriek, and then the creature's head disappeared. Its claws went slack on my thighs, but I was still stuck to its chest.

My lungs were burning and spots floated before my eyes. The dead weight of the each-uisge was pulling me down. I had a panicky moment as I started to inhale some water. With every ounce of power left in my arms, I swam up to the surface. Just as I thought I would never reach it, I broke through. The air hurt as I gasped. I floundered for a moment before Caimbeul grabbed me by my collar and pulled me from the water.

He laid me, none too gently, on the stony bank. I coughed up water and hacked out some bile. My legs felt heavy, and I realized the each-uisge was still stuck to them.

"Cut it off," I said.

"That won't work. You'll have pieces of it stuck to your pants forever."

"Well, it's better than dragging the whole thing along with me," I said, coughing up more water.

"Take off your pants," he said.

"Oh, fragging hell," I said. I unbuttoned my jeans and skinned them off. It took a while between the wet and the each-uisge.

"And so that was the test?" he asked.

"N-n-no," I stammered. My teeth were chattering and gooseflesh had broken out over my body. "T-t-that was a warning. They're serious about the test."

"Well," he said, looking chagrined that he hadn't helped, "we'd better get you out of those wet things."

He wrapped his arms around me. I let myself lean against him and take in his warmth and scent. It was good to be there, if only for a moment.

*She can't move. Legs and arms like lead. But she
hears . . . things.*

Things rustling beyond her line of sight.

Things with evil intentions.

10

"What next?" Caimbeul asked.

I was sitting in the back seat of the car pulling dry
clothes on. My coat and boots were ruined, so I
wadded them up in a towel I'd taken from the hotel.
Under normal circumstances I wouldn't have in-
dulged in that sort of petty larceny, but these weren't
normal times.

Caimbeul was driving. We were heading south-
west away from The Burren. I pulled a heavy gray
sweater over my head, then slid on black jeans.
Sneakers were next, after which I climbed over the
front seat to the passenger side.

"Better?" he asked.

"Drier, at least," I replied. "But that brackish
smell is going to stay with me for a while."

"Not just you."

"My apologies," I said. "Next time a each-uisge
decides to have me for a snack I'll be sure to tell it
not to get you wet at the same time."

"I'd appreciate that," he replied.

"*De nada,* babycakes."

"You know I hate it when you call me babycakes."

"Like I said, 'Life is . . .' "

"I know. I know."

We stopped in a small town south of The Burren for food. It was fast approaching dusk and I wanted to be out in the countryside as soon as possible. The air was tanged with sea salt and humidity. Though it wasn't that cold, the damp seemed to seep into my bones, making them ache.

Leaving the car at the restaurant where we'd eaten, we walked to the edge of the town. The road out of town was little more than dirt and cobblestones. It had played hell on the suspension of the rental. I imagined Caimbeul was making a running ledger in his head of all the expenses of the trip. When this penurious streak had come on him I didn't know.

"Look," he said, grabbing my arm and pointing. Off to one side of the road was a grove of trees. It was shaded purple and gray in the twilight. A fog had rolled in from the sea and made everything look fuzzy and insubstantial. Surrounding the grove were a series of tiny flickering lights that bobbed and floated three meters above the ground.

Then I heard the faint, delicate tones of music. A flute and recorder, I thought. Perhaps a viola thrown in there.

"Ignis fatuus," I said. "Will-o'-the-wisps."

The flower necklace I'd made while we were walking The Burren was waterlogged, but still serviceable. I'd rescued it from my coat after we'd reached the car. Now I put it around my neck.

"I can't believe you're using that," Caimbeul said.

"Whatever works."

"Primrose necklaces to reveal faeries?"

"Yes," I said. "And you'd better put yours on. I don't want to lose you."

He snorted.

"I know it hasn't occurred to you before, Harlequin," I said. "But you don't know everything. Some magic isn't complex—some is made up of simple things. And sometimes, that's the most potent magic. Because it's so obvious that everyone overlooks it."

"But I thought this was to allow *humans* to see faerie," he said.

"Oh, come now," I replied. "How many humans were ever able to see faerie without their permission, help or no? No, this magic is from before human memory."

He pulled the necklace from his pocket. It was wilted and droopy. With a sigh, he slipped it over his neck. It hung there limp and pathetic, faded green and pink against his black leather jacket.

Sucker.

I hid my smile and went back to following the lights. Every time I thought we were about to catch up, they moved away. This went on until my patience began to wear thin. Then, all at once, we were at the top of a hill.

A group of oak trees stood to one side, their leaves mostly gone. A circle of toadstools ringed around the trees. Inside the ring, the lights flickered and bobbed about. They melted and changed shape, and eventually I saw what I had come for.

Dancing around the ring were an assortment of the strange and fearful creatures of faerie. Please, no laughing. I know that in recent times the idea of faerie has come to mean something other, and much more pleasant, than what it really was. But since the Awakening, I suspect that Disney notion has flown out the door.

For the most part they were dressed in rags or pieces of plants. Their thin, sinewy bodies were pulled and bent into grotesque shapes. With their mouths opened to smile, they revealed rows of sharp, pointed teeth. Some sported wings while others had antennae flowing back from their brows. They all had the pointed ears that we elves share. Giving rise, no doubt, to the rumors that they are our descendants.

Spriggans danced with leprechauns while fir darrigs tripped the unwary. Goblins and pixies tried to swing each other out of the circle. They whirled and danced and laughed. The shadows they cast flickered and strobed. It was Dante's vision of Hell.

One of the dancers broke from the group and ran over to us. It grabbed my hand and pulled me forward.

"Welcome, mother," it said. "We've been waiting for you."

"What of my friend?" I asked.

"He is of no account right now."

We were in the center of the ring. The sharp, wizened faces of the faeries jerked in and out of shadow. I had thought they were much smaller than me at first, but now I saw we were the same height. Or perhaps I was shrinking. Like Alice.

My feet moved along with the music now. I looked down and saw my jeans and sweater were gone, replaced by a long flowing gown made of silver silk. We spun around and around and suddenly . . .

I am on the deck of a large ship. It floats in the sky. Magic propels it. Magic that brings both good and evil to this world.

I'm dancing here.

Dancing with trolls. We sail through the dark night sky, laughing and dancing like children. One of the trolls is old and wizened. He wears a long robe embroidered with patterns. His flesh is wrinkled and thick like an elephant's. But he is kind. And he is my friend.

The faces of these trolls flash before me, the memory of them clear and bright as day. I'd thought I'd forgotten them. But no, that was just a story I told myself.

Now I'm standing on the deck of the ship. It is the afternoon. The ship is in the middle of a battle. The trolls are fighting, but where is my friend? I go to look for him.

I find him below-deck lying in a pool of blood. He's broken his leg. I have some knowledge of healing and I try to help him. But I've brought more than my healing magic along on this trip. I've brought him: Ysrthgrathe.

I know what happens next. I've played it out in my head so many times that I think I've grown numb from it.

But I'm wrong.

There are some things you never get used to.

The faeries danced around me, laughing. Cruel tricks are their stock and trade.

"Did you like the dance, mother?" one of the spriggans asked.

I couldn't answer because there was no breath in my chest. Tears stung my eyes. But I kept dancing.

I couldn't stop.

There's a car. She's driving it through rain-slicked streets. The headlights make yellow beams against the oily pavement. There's no other traffic. Everything is deserted.

She stops for a red light. There's a tap against the passenger-side glass. She looks up. A pockmarked face appears at the window, broken fingernails trail across the wetness down to the door handle. Too late, she realizes that the doors are unlocked.

She can't keep him out.

11

Where was Caimbeul?

I couldn't stop dancing now. This was part of it. Part of the test. And perhaps a bit of revenge at the same time. I know they thought they had just cause, but that was part of the past, too.

I looked down and saw that my dress had changed again. Glamour. Nasty tricks of the first water. I wore a long white dress made of rose petals. Not unlike the ones Alachia had favored in Blood Wood.

I open my eyes. The faeries are gone. As I look about, I notice that the trees have died. They are nothing more than hollowed-out stumps. It's cold.

Colder than it should be this time of year. Or anytime in Tír na nÓg.

Looking up, I see that the sky has turned the color of old oysters. And the air smells of burnt flesh.

I start to run down the hill, back to the town where Caimbeul and I left the car. The fields I run through are fallow, dead, and brown. Where there was once a cobblestone road, now only small jagged pieces of stone show against the dun-colored earth.

A stillness hangs in the air. But this is not the silence of a quiet afternoon.

The buildings I pass are crumbling. Finally, I come to the tavern where we stopped for lunch. No vehicles are parked outside. The windows are boarded up, but the door hangs open, listing on one hinge.

I go inside.

It takes a moment for my eyes to adjust to the dark. Broken chairs litter the floor. Glass crunches under my feet. There's no one here.

I walk outside again.

All around me, everything crumbles to dust.

And I am alone.

Tears streamed down my face. The spriggans grabbed my hands and spun me about harder and faster. The world revolved around me until all I saw was a blur of light and motion. Shutting my eyes, I tried to block it out.

I open my eyes.

We spin about under the azure sky, hands locked with one another.

"Faster," he says.

"You'll make yourself sick," I reply.

"Faster."

So we turn and turn until we both fall down onto the soft grass.

"The sky is spinning," he says.

I put my hand on his forehead. He is warm, but not unusually so. My hand looks so large against his tiny forehead. I can hardly believe that this creature, this small boy, came from me.

He pushes my hand away, impatient again to be going. In a flash he is up and off and running. Chubby legs pump and I see he's beginning to lose his baby fat. In another few months he'll be a little boy, a baby no longer. And I find I can't bear the idea of his growing older. I would keep him like this forever.

From high in the sky, a bird cries out. I look up, shadowing my eyes with my hand. It begins a slow descent, circling around and around. Black with yellow wing-tips.

I hear a shout and turn. The sky has turned dark as ink and rain slices down.

Standing next to our small stone house are my son and an old man. Somehow I have missed something. Something important, something I must understand. Then the man drags my son into the house. The door slams shut. An eternity passes, and then a crimson pool seeps slowly under the door.

Tears ran down my face.

"Mother, did we make you weep?" asked one of

the spriggans. He looked at me with a concerned expression, then burst into laughter.

"No, no," said another. "She only cries for her *dead* children. The rest of us must shift for ourselves."

"That's enough of this nonsense," I said loudly. I was having trouble breathing. After all, I was getting awfully old for this sort of thing. "This is a ridiculous game. Tell me what I need to know. Now."

This caused nothing but giggles from them.

"You know it's no good demanding anything from us," they said. "We always do what we will. Disobedient children."

And then they spun me around faster.

The room is spinning. The fire in the hearth is hot and I feel as though it's burning my bare skin. I'm burning up. Hotter and hotter until I think I'll go mad from it. Maybe I already have.

Pain blossoms bright inside me. I shut my eyes and see red against black. Hands touch me trying to soothe, but it is no use. There are some things for which there is no balm.

Then the pain is over. They bring me something bundled up.

I hold my arms out to receive this gift. I pull back the blanket. Inside is a horrible apparition.

"This is not my baby," I cry. "What have you done with my baby?"

They take the bundle away from me.

"It's a changeling," says one in a voice she thinks

is too soft for me to hear. "The faeries have stolen her baby."

"You can't blame us, Mother," said the spriggan. "That was your own doing."

"Oh, be quiet," I snapped. The spriggan skulked away.

Sweat ran down my face. I was growing tired of their games.

"Tell me where they are," I said.

"Patience, Mother," they replied.

I'm running away. The earth rushes below me as I fly. Cradled in my arms is a child. This is no changeling, but my own flesh and blood.

At last we come to our home. Inside, the air is stale and musty. But that doesn't matter because we are home and safe.

The storms come. Rain pounds against the roof and makes the windows rattle. But we don't mind, we're warm and dry. Then I remember, someone is coming. Coming for us.

The door slams open. He is here. But he's not the real threat. I don't realize this until it's too late.

Foolish foolish woman.

Something jerked me.

Someone.

Caimbeul had hauled me from the dance. Looking down, I saw I no longer wore the petal gown. Just my own gray sweater and black jeans. Orange streaks colored the sky to the east.

"Why did you do that?" I asked.

"I just now found you."

"What?"

"You went running off, and I couldn't find you for three days," he said angrily. "Do you think I enjoyed tramping all over this jerkwater place? I used up a hell of a lot of goodwill trying to figure out where they took you. Not to mention the energy."

"Thanks," I said.

"Thanks? Thanks. She said, 'Thanks.' Is that it?"

He was beginning to annoy me. I was searching the ground trying to see if they'd left anything behind for me to go on. And all he was doing was blathering away.

"Yes, thanks for coming after me. What do you want, Harlequin?"

"Perhaps some gratitude," he said. "I've been all over Connaught looking for you. It's taken a hell of a lot of casting to locate you."

"I hope you're up to some more," I said.

"Why?" A suspicious look crossed his face.

"Because the only way I know now to reach the Court is by calling up the Hunt."

He looked a little pale. I was glad to see he still had some respect for the old ways.

"The Chasse Artu?"

"Yes," I said, feeling a little happier at the thought. "The Wild Hunt. It's been so long since I've called one, let alone two. We really must make preparations."

"Are you mad? You can't possibly call up the Hunt yourself," he said. There was a frightened look in his eye. "It would take more power than you or I possess, even combined, not to mention the time involved."

I smiled. "Of course I can't call up the entire Hunt myself. No one could. But I can bring up the steeds. Come along. I'll sleep while you drive. By the way, where are we?"

There is a barren plain. No grass grows here. No tree mars the vastness of land. Only the long unbroken earth stretching out beneath the sickly yellow sky.

A moon hangs large and low. It casts a green glow and turns her skin the color of illness.

Of death.

12

When I woke, it was getting near dark. The sun rested low on the horizon, showing its face for the first time since we'd come to the Tír. Caimbeul had turned the vid to some music station as he drove. The vid flickered and changed, turning his pale face a rainbow of colors.

It took me a moment to orient myself. I felt groggy and irritated at the sensation. My scalp itched and my eyes felt gritty. A few hours of sleep to make up for the three days I'd missed weren't enough.

"Where are we?" I asked.

"Just south of Galway City," he replied.

"Has it changed much?" I asked.

"Has what changed?"

"Galway City."

"Compared to what?"

"Compared to what it was before the Awakening."

"A bit," he said. "The old ways have taken hold pretty firmly there."

I pulled my bag out from under the front seat and began rummaging through it. Gum wrappers, cigarettes, shoelaces—then I found it: a small tin whistle. It rode on a thin copper necklace that I slipped over my head and nestled down between my breasts. I looked out at the passing countryside.

It had gone wild here. No fences marked property lines. The roads were mostly unpaved, little more than dirt ruts. It reminded me of a time long ago, long before this world. Back when another world was young. No, it was me who was young then.

I remembered what happened in that place so long ago. How could I ever forget? And now it seemed that the mistakes of the past would be repeated. This world would be torn apart unless I stopped them. Unless I stopped him.

Just as the sun was setting, I saw the place. Stone tombs silhouetted against the red sky.

"Pull over here," I said.

Caimbeul slowed the car.

"Are you sure?" he asked. "I can't feel anything . . ."

"It'll do. This place is lousy with cairns. The whole area is Awakened."

A blast of cool air hit me when I opened the car door. The magic was heavy here. It made the hair on the back of my neck stand on end. Then I noticed a strange feeling I hadn't had in a time out of mind:

excitement. Things couldn't be worse, yet I felt alive for the first time in years. Had the centuries finally worn me down? I knew they had for some of the others. Some until they resorted to terrible means to stop the emptiness.

But I had a reason to live. I knew my purpose. It was a sacred task. To keep the world safe. To protect it. To protect the people in it. Or so I'd told myself.

As I started for the tombs, Caimbeul grabbed my arm.

"Are you certain this is the only way?" he asked.

I turned and looked at him. In the flat red twilight his face looked like the very vision of Lucifer. A dark, yet beautiful, angel.

"Why, Caimbeul, I almost think you care," I said.

He frowned. "Don't be flip," he said. "If Ysrth-grathe has found you . . . how can you be safe?"

I reached up and touched his face. I can't describe how it felt, only that it felt like him. Like Caimbeul. My flesh remembered his as surely as it might remember the smoothness of velvet or the scratch of sandpaper.

"Nothing is safe anymore," I replied. "Besides, I've been alive for so long, it might be good to rest. Don't you ever want to just . . . stop?"

"No," he said. An angry look crossed his face, and he pulled away from me. "It's always better to be alive. Life is better than death."

I wanted to stay and argue with him, but there was no time. It almost made me laugh. After so many years, to have no time.

Instead, I turned and began walking to the cairns.

The sun had disappeared and the sky was fading from scarlet into plum. The wind had died down, and the air was still. No birds sang. No leaves rustled. No animal noises carried to me.

Once I reached the cairns, I turned to see if Caimbeul had followed me. He was a shadow against the fading light. I held my hands out to him and, after a moment, he took them. Though I didn't need him to call up the Hunt, I wanted him to be there with me.

I closed my eyes and relaxed. In my youth, I had learned magic as part of the fabric of life. I saw it not as a force to be manipulated, but as integral to life itself. A thread broken here could cause something there to unravel. Pulling threads together could create something where there had been nothing.

But the mages today saw magic as something else. Their way of seeing the world was strange and alien to me. I objected to any kind of cybernetic enhancement. Machines can't create. They can only do what they're told.

As I began to chant the words to the spell, I opened my eyes. The moon was dark and the stars had yet to appear. I couldn't see Caimbeul's face, but could just make out the shape of him before me.

My eyes adjusted, and gradually I could see again. The granite of the cairns glowed ghostly pale. Caimbeul's face looked as though it floated in the air, unattached to his body. He joined me in saying the words to the spell. It was a strange duet, our words conjuring up the Hunt. I blew the whistle, and it made no sound that either I or anyone else in this world could hear.

At first there was nothing but our voices breaking the silence. Then the wind began. It howled across the open fields and whistled through the tombs. Caimbeul's hair was pulled free of his ponytail and whipped across his face. The ground began to tremble.

The magic flowed through me. Into me. It filled me and shook me. My muscles screamed with the agony of trying to hold this power. To mold it to my will. Sweat broke out across my face. It ran down my back and streamed over my breasts.

It was terrible, this force. This chaos and madness which threatened to engulf me. It wracked my muscles. I felt as though it would rip me apart. Tear from me my soul. That it would allow the insanity of the past to come and claim me again.

In the distance I could hear the thundering of hooves. I raised my voice, barely able to hear myself. Barely able to force the words from my throat. Caimbeul's words were snatched away by the wind as he uttered them.

The magic trembled in me, flew around me, pulled at the world and drew things from me. Terrible things. Apparitions from the past. Nightmares from the future. We stood there, trembling, and chanted the old words. Words of power. Until our voices grew hoarse and our throats were raw and our legs would barely support us.

At last we stopped.

Abruptly, the air was still and silent.

I released Caimbeul's hand and turned.

Below us, at the base of the hill where the cairns stood, was what we'd called.

They looked up at us expectantly. Their eyes reflected red iridescence. Black coats melted into black night.

In the distance, I heard the howling of the hounds and wolves. The gabriel ratchets. Their cries were lonely, as though they realized that they'd been abandoned by the steeds which led them. At their head was a tall, cloaked form. Though I knew that this was the apparition who tended the beasts, its appearance was so close to Ysrthgrathe's that, for a moment, I thought my enemy had come for me.

A long, bony arm appeared from the depths of the apparition's cloak. It beckoned us. I glanced for a moment at Caimbeul. His lips were set in a hard line.

"You don't have to come," I said.

"What?" he replied. "And miss all the fun?"

At the bottom of the hill we were gestured to two horses. These were the horses of the ancient Tuatha de Danaan. Created from fire, not earth, and able to live for hundreds of years. I had not ridden one in a thousand years.

As we tried to mount the horses, they began to dance away and reached back every now and again to nip us with their long, yellow teeth. I grabbed a handful of long mane to help pull myself up. I hoped I would have enough strength left in me for the ride I knew was ahead.

There was no noise as we mounted. No rattle of harnesses. No sound at all. I turned to the master of the horses, who stood looking at me. "To the Seelie Court," I shouted over the din. The apparition nodded.

Just then, I had a strange tingling sensation, as if someone unseen was watching me. I looked around, and there, in the distance, atop one of the far hills, were the hounds, stags and wolves. They swirled together, writhing like a thousand snakes, and disappeared from my sight. I shuddered at their terrible power.

The horses lunged forward, jerking us in our seats. From then on we were no longer in control. As if we ever truly had been.

We thundered down bare fields and into muddy flats. Fences were hurdled without a falter. Streams and meadows slipped away. Sparks flew as hooves struck rocky expanses. Lather foamed up on the horses, but they never slowed. My cheeks became chilled and chapped; my hands ached from holding onto the reins. Tears streamed from my eyes.

We overtook cars on the road, causing accidents. Still we did not slow.

Then we were at the shore. We pounded across the sand, plumes of it spraying into the air. Then into the tide, never slowing as we rode up and over the water. Galloping across the top of the ocean as though it were a puddle.

Across the water I saw a misty turquoise glow. As we came closer, I saw that there was an island surrounded by this light. In moments we were on the beach thundering across the sand.

This was not one of the Aran Islands, for we had passed those as we sped across the bay. This was one of the isles of fable. From legends I had helped create and had forgotten in the long expanse of time.

This place must be Hy-Breasail, the island believed to rise from the sea only once every seven years. I barely had time to realize this before the Horses surged across the beach and went crashing into the forest.

A path opened up before us. Whether it was there to begin with or the Horses created it as they went, I cannot say. The trail began to climb upward. We plunged on through the forest, shattering the silence with our passing. At last we burst forth into a great open plain and stopped.

Though it was autumn in Tír na nÓg, here spring held sway. I could smell it in the air, could feel the warm and gentle caress of the breeze. It was balm to my sore, chapped face.

I looked about and saw a castle perched on a cliff above us. So much a part of the island it was that there was no telling where the castle began and the rock it sat upon ended. As I watched, lights appeared on the pathway below the castle. They bobbed and floated downward toward us.

Closer and closer they came, and we waited for them, silent and patient.

At last they appeared on the edge of the clearing, riming it in gold and silver light.

Such a congregation of the Sleagh Maith. It almost made me forget my own mission, so good was it to gaze upon them again. The sprites and spriggans, brownies and hags, boogies, leprechauns, gnomes, and goblins all clustered around, throwing their crooked shadows against the rocky cliff behind them.

I could hear their shrill cries and nasty whispers. They knew who I was even if there were those who would have it otherwise. There was but a moment for these impressions. They parted and a procession of elves appeared. Each was dressed in tight-fitting dun-colored leather garments. Some had tattoos marking their arms and faces. Others had datajacks glistening in shaved skulls. I ignored them as they surrounded us.

I glanced over at Caimbeul. He was a bit paler than normal, but after the night we'd had so far, that was to be expected. He looked up at me and gave a little smile. I found myself smiling back, oddly happy at that moment.

"This is hardly a laughing matter," came a voice from beyond the edge of the faerie light. All the elves and faeries bowed down immediately. I squinted into the darkness. A ghost-like form moved forward. As it stepped into the ring of light, I saw that it was a woman. She was dressed in a white flowing gown. Her fiery hair was pulled back severely from her face, but left to cascade down her back almost to her heels. The brilliant blue eyes were unchanged. The skin as pale and white as milk.

Alachia.

Silence stretched out between us. I hadn't seen her in the flesh since 1941.

"So," she said at last. "You've come. And the hard way, too."

"Well, we can't all have the prerogatives of age. I wish to speak to Lady Brane Deigh," I said. "She rules here now."

Alachia smiled. It was chilling.

"Power is a fluid thing," she said. "You'd do well to remember that."

Once that sort of remark from her would have frightened me. But that was far in the past. Now there was a larger threat at work. Not just to me, but to the survival of the world. And then, I was older now, too.

"Perhaps you should mind your own advice," I said. "You've let so much pass through your own hands."

"Caimbeul," she said brightly, ignoring my last remark. "How good it is to see you again. But really, you need to improve your choice of companions. You know what they say about the company you keep."

She slipped past me and took his arm, leading him away from me toward the castle.

"Do come, Aina," she called over her shoulder. "We mustn't keep Lady Brane waiting."

I watched her lead him into the night until all I saw was the white blur of her dress.

She opens her eyes. The world is upside-down. No, it's her perspective that's off. But isn't that always the way of it?

Sitting up, she sees that she's been lying on the ground. The fall leaves covering her rustle and slide away, revealing her naked body. How she came to be here in this wood she doesn't remember. But she thinks she should know.

Then comes the pain.

It burns and stings like a thousand hornets. Her skin is on fire and she cannot stop it. As she looks on, small, round welts appear on her flesh. Sharp points burst through the welts, puckering the skin.

Thorns.

13

No mortal being could have traversed the path to Lady Brane Deigh's castle. But then, it wasn't designed for mortals. The Sleagh Meath loved anything that might confuse or baffle mortals and so took great delight in the corkscrew turns, disappearing paths, and other annoying tricks to fool the unwary traveler.

But I had seen all these games before. The Seelie Court was but another incarnation of something much older and more sinister. How many of them remembered, or even knew, the full story?

Politics was a tricky business, and I'd done my best to stay out of it for most of my life. But now it seemed I had no choice. I was the only one who appeared to be willing to take the chance. No, I was the only one willing to see the threat of the Enemy for what it was—the ruination of the world.

I had to grasp hold of this thought because all my old fears came back to me in this place. Once I foolishly thought that power would protect me from harm. How I discovered the error of that belief is another tale.

For now, I kept up with Alachia's lead. She glided over the rocks as though they weren't there. Each turn was taken with a casual nonchalance, and all the while I could hear her keeping up a steady banter with Caimbeul.

I knew their history was a long one, and I wondered if she knew how much my life had been entwined with his. And how far back it extended. Part of me hoped she didn't know, relishing the secret. And a part wanted her to know. Wanted her to know that even when she wielded so much power that most of my people trembled before her, I had won a small victory over her.

But there was no more time to wonder over such childish things—we had reached the gate of the castle.

Alachia waved and the gates swung silently inward. The courtyard was bathed in the light from thousands of floating will-o'-the-wisps. They fluttered around us, rising and falling with the breeze. It was like walking through a rain of stars.

Then we were moving up the wide, white, marble steps leading to the great doors. Made of oak and tall as a two-story house, they were banded in brass in deference to the faerie hatred of iron. As the doors opened, a radiance spilled forth. I stepped into the brilliance.

The great hall of the castle dwarfed any I had seen before or since. This was no mean feat given what I've seen in my time. I could feel the magical energies flowing through this place. The magic to pull Hy-Breasail from the sea, to create this castle upon it, to gather the members of faerie who still remained here on Earth, and to pull back those who had left for other planes. An impressive feat indeed.

At the far end of the hall, I saw a group of elves. Alachia moved toward them with her usual single-mindedness. As she approached, the group parted and allowed her to pass. I squeezed in just as they closed ranks again.

Standing at the center of all this attention was a tall elf wearing a black leather breast plate over a long white dress. Her fine hair was bobbed off short, one side shorn away so short I could see the fragile shape of her skull beneath. Her skin was the color of amber and I saw that her eyes were blue, transparent and glittering as ice. Though she was only as tall as Alachia, there emanated from her a power that I found compelling. The same sort of power that Alachia had once wielded so many lives ago.

She glanced at Alachia, then at Caimbeul, and finally, at me.

"Lady Brane, may I present Aina Sluage," said Caimbeul. Alachia shot him a hateful look, but didn't say anything.

I stepped forward, but didn't bow. Though I knew she was made as I, she was only a child compared to me. Just as I was a child compared to Alachia. And even if she did hold sway over this court, she did so at the sufferance of myself and the other Elders. So, instead of bowing, I offered her my hand. For a moment, I thought she might not take it, but then her smooth, cool hand was in mine. I felt an odd shock, and then our eyes met.

Yes, she was fit to rule, I saw. Though I had abstained from participating in the new politics between the Tirs, I was glad to know that there was someone strong enough to deal with whatever was to come. The only question was: Could I convince her that the threat was real?

"I have heard your name," Lady Brane said. Her voice was sweet as summer wine. "When I was younger I almost thought you were a ghost, invented to scare children."

So that was to be the way of it. Well, I'd handled worse in my time.

She released my hand, then beckoned me to her side as she turned to leave the group. I heard the murmuring of the others as we passed, but I ignored it. Alachia's face was even paler than normal and I saw her eyes narrow as we passed. *Good,* I thought. *Let her worry a bit.* I suspected the nature of the poison she had managed to spread about me while I was gone worrying about more important matters.

"You've created quite a stir," she said. "Calling up the Hunt's horses. A most impressive feat. And, from what I understand, only you and Harlequin were present."

"That is correct," I said. "There are those of us ... who are of an age ... who have found such things to be ... within our grasp." I looked around for Caimbeul, surprised to see him hanging back. It was so unlike him.

She stared ahead, leading me toward the back of the hall. I caught the scent of her perfume. A complex scent: grasses, sandalwood, and a few other notes of which I couldn't be certain. Elusive.

"And why did you call the Chasse Artu?" she asked.

"I have been away a long time," I said. "I needed to find the Court."

"Yes," she replied. "I thought as much. No other way would have found us so quickly. We have been careful for a while now. But you come to us with the toss of a spell so powerful it would take half my court to cast it. I see some of what I've heard is true."

We had come to the back half of the hall. A great feast was laid out. Row after row of tables were covered with white linen, fine gold eating utensils, and bone china. Garlands of flowers were swagged onto the tablecloths. Most of the tables were filled with members of the Sleagh Meath and Awakened elves.

Invisible hands served and took away platters of food and jugs of wine.

Lady Brane led me to a raised table in the center of all the others. She took a seat and motioned me to take mine next to her. As I sat down, I noticed Caimbeul finding a place down at Alachia's end of the table and I wondered how best to approach the reason for my visit. I didn't know precisely what lies Alachia had spread about me. My cup was filled with wine, and food appeared on my plate. I didn't eat. Couldn't.

Lady Brane, however, was having no such problems. She drank heavily from her cup and tucked away the feast like she'd been starving for a year. All this was done with a grace and delicacy that made it look like the most delightful thing I'd ever witnessed.

"You aren't eating," she said with a little frown. "Is the food not to your liking?"

I pushed a pea with my fork and shook my head. "No, thank you. I'm not hungry. Lady Brane," I said. "I am not a threat to the Seelie Court, nor to you."

She turned and looked at me, her expression unreadable.

"And what makes you think I find you threatening?" she asked.

"I just assumed that you had been told ... things," I said. Good, Aina, I thought, stick your foot in it right off.

She picked up a pear and bit into it. I could smell the sweet aroma of it. It took her a few moments to finish off the pear. Daintily, she dabbed at her mouth with a napkin before speaking again.

"Yes," she said. "I have heard stories. From several sources. You have not endeared yourself to many of the Elders. But there are other, more powerful, voices who seem to value you. So, I decided I should see for myself what sort of creature you are."

"What sort of creature?" I said. "That hardly sounds impartial. Unlike Alachia, the politics of men have little interest for me. But your court deals with matters that do concern me. Magic and mysticism have long been intertwined for our people."

She shrugged. "Perhaps some of what I've heard does concern me," she said. "I am proud of being an elf and I am proud of our Tír. It has come to my attention that you have chosen others over your own kind in past disputes."

Alachia's fine Italian hand at work, no doubt.

"Yes," I said. "There was a time when I had to make that painful choice. But there were reasons for my choice and I was not the only one who made that decision. I, too, am proud of my people. But we are not perfect, nor are we always right. I am not blindly devoted to every act. And those matters have no bearing on the dangers before us now."

Lady Brane took a sip from her glass, then swirled the contents around as she stared into them.

"Yes," she said at last. "These dangers. How is it you know of them and the rest of us do not? Are you so special? So powerful?"

Yes, I wanted to say. Yes, *I am special. I haven't*

*forgotten why I am here. I haven't forgotten the past.
If that makes me special, then so be it. As for power,
how could I have survived for almost eight thousand
years without it?* But of course I said none of this.
She would discover in her own time what a curse
immortality was.

"Perhaps it would be easier if we were to discuss
this in a less public place," I said. "There are some
things that should only be spoken of in private."

"You're right," she said. "I was hoping only to
come to a quick resolution of this matter."

"That is my most fervent wish," I said.

"Very well," she said. "Come with me. You, Harlequin, Alachia, and I will discuss this matter."

I rose, and without even a backward glance at
Caimbeul, I followed her from the hall. It had been
a long time since I'd had to call upon the good
graces of my fellow elves. I suspected the reception
to what I was about to say would be chilly indeed.

She opens her eyes. Darkness suffocates her, pushing against her like an old lover. Putting her hands up, she feels the smoothness of satin. She pushes, but there is resistance. A hardness under the soft fabric.

A spell. There is light.

This is no kaer. This is a coffin.

And she's been buried alive in it.

14

Lady Brane motioned for me to sit. The room was an odd mixture of magic, antiques, and hardware. Though I dislike the technology that Caimbeul so adores, even I was impressed with the array of hyper-edged toys. Any shadowrunner would have been drooling at the chance to get his hands on Lady Deigh's high-tech toys.

I didn't sit. Instead I wandered about the room, looking at the collection of elven artifacts. Encased in a glass box was a long silver sword whose hasp was plated in gold and set with cabochon emeralds and rubies. So, this was where the Sword of Nuadha had finally come to rest. I thought it had been lost long ago.

Next to it was a plain cup roughly carved from

horn. It should have seemed prosaic, sitting there next to the glory of the sword, but it was the other way round. The Sword of Nuadha seemed coarse and obvious.

I'd just stepped over to a lovely painting of Caimbeul in some costume I didn't recognize when he and Alachia came into the room. Lady Brane smiled at her and she smiled back. My heart sank when I saw this. Already I was at a disadvantage. I could only hope that Caimbeul would provide a strong argument for my position.

"Now that we're all here," began Lady Brane. "Shouldn't we start?"

"You are the only Elders?" I asked, more than a little shocked.

"No, of course not," said Lady Brane. "But the others have agreed to let me handle this situation as I see fit. They have deferred to Lady Alachia and me."

I glanced over at Caimbeul, who kept his face blank. And I wondered if he knew this would be the situation going in.

"Very well," I said. "It's really quite simple. The Horrors have returned."

Alachia let out a silvery laugh that I just knew would enchant any man who heard it and which set my teeth on edge.

"You are still so melodramatic, Aina," she said. "Good heavens. It is far too early for them to have returned."

When I answered and my voice was calm, it surprised me. For as long as I could remember, Alachia had the power to anger me with her flip comments.

"I realize that you are far older than I," I said. "But my experience with what you so blithely refer to as the Enemy is hardly inconsiderable. Even you would have to admit that."

She gave a small nod of her head, the best acknowledgment I could hope for.

"Caimbeul came to me the other day and told me of his recent experience with them."

Alachia and Lady Brane looked at him expectantly, and he preened a bit under the attention. What an ego. But he did manage to tell them about Thayla and the bridge from the astral planes and how he had stopped them.

"Well," said Alachia. "There you have it. Thayla's there protected by one of those hirelings, and we're all quite safe."

"Are you completely mad?" I asked, losing my temper at last. "Hasn't anything he's said sunk in? Oh, I expected him to be full of beer and sausages. He's always had this messiah complex, but you know better. If they don't get through that way, they'll find another. They're coming back now because they *can*. Look at what happened in Maui."

And then it dawned on me. I almost hit myself for being such a fool. Of course, she knew the dangers. But she didn't care. I thought back over our history together and realized that Alachia had been at her most powerful during the times when we faced the Enemy. Her dark knowledge had been as much a bane as help. But it hadn't mattered because we would do anything to survive. And I knew what she wanted was for that time to come again. She was tired of waiting.

But perhaps I could reach Lady Brane.

"Lady Brane," I began, "I know you have heard terrible stories about me. Some are even true. But that isn't what is important here. What is important is that I'm telling the truth. I know better than most the evil these creatures will unleash should they come through before we are prepared. They will lay waste the world and everything in it. And this time we aren't prepared to stop them. We haven't the power."

"You seem powerful enough," said Lady Brane. "You call down the Hunt, or part of it, at least. You live beyond the rule of either Tir. You consort with the Great Worms as though you were one of them instead of one of us."

"Now, now," said Alachia. "Let's be fair. Aina has always been very forthright about what she believes in. She has never challenged the authority of the Tirs. Nor has she sought temporal power for herself. I prefer to think that she has been terribly misled and will someday see her error and come back to us."

I looked at Caimbeul, trying hard not to lose what little I'd had to eat in the last few days. The expression on his face was shocked, then suspicious. Yet, still he didn't speak up. What was wrong with him?

"Alachia is right, of course," said Lady Brane. "What other proof do you have that the Enemy is near?"

"Dreams," I said, hoping she would understand the importance of this. "And the certain knowledge that one of the most powerful of them is already among us."

"And where is this dread creature?" asked Alachia.

"I know not," I said. "Only that he is here now. He has contacted me."

"And why would it bother to come for you?"

"Because," I said. "It knows me. I am the one it wants."

"And you are so special?"

"Yes," I said. "You should remember. It was the monster who marked me so many millennia ago."

I thought I saw Alachia go a little paler. Lady Brane seemed a bit confused, and I suspected there was much that Alachia had left out of her history lessons.

"How do you know for certain that it is this one?" Alachia asked. "This could be the work of another Elder. You have your enemies, my dear."

My eyes narrowed. "I know of no enemy of mine who would use such matters for the Game. That would be a gross breach of etiquette. No, it is he."

"But what would you have us do about it?" Alachia asked. "It seems that this is really your problem."

"Now, perhaps," I said. "But it means they can get through. We are not safe any more. We must prepare for them, and also curtail our use of magic."

Lady Brane came out of her chair. "Stop using magic? Now I think you are the one who is mad," she said. "I hardly think one of these creatures is a serious enough threat to us. You are terribly powerful. Why don't you just kill it?"

"I've tried," I said bleakly. "I thought I had rid the world of him long ago. But I was mistaken. That is why it is vital for us to put a stop to them now—before they get a better foothold in the world."

"How are you going to stop everyone from using magic?" asked Lady Brane.

"It isn't small magics that are the danger. It's the great acts that draw them. The Great Ghost Dance. The Veil, I'm certain, is creating a pull. While it will protect you from them, it will also bring them like carrion to a carcass."

"Not a very appetizing thought," muttered Alachia.

"You know what a danger they are," I said. "Why haven't you told her?"

"I have told her. But I've also told her we dealt successfully with them before."

Caimbeul and I both laughed—harsh and sarcastic.

"Did Alachia tell you what was done to survive?" I asked Lady Brane.

"Not yet," Alachia said coldly. "What difference does it make now? We survived."

"Do you think Aithne would agree with you?" I asked.

"Perhaps. Perhaps not. But he would no doubt agree with me long before he would agree with you."

I turned away and walked to a small tray set up in

one corner of the room. Bottles filled with amber, gold, and red liquid glowed softly. I pickcd one at random and splashed a healthy amount into one of the cut crystal glasses. It burned going down. Irish whiskey.

"I have a proposal," said Lady Brane. "Though I am inclined with Alachia to think you are overestimating the threat of this creature, I do not wish to completely disregard your warning. You are, after all, one of the Elders. And you have not meddled in our affairs unnecessarily.

"So I suggest that you go to Tir Tairngire. Though we are at cross-purposes with them in many things, this matter could certainly constitute a danger that concerns the entire elven nation. If you can convince the Elders there that the threat is real, then I shall lend you any support you might need."

A politician's answer, but better than none. Or an unequivocal "no."

"Thank you, Lady Brane," I said. "I see the Tír chose well in you."

A little flattery never hurt.

"Yes," said Alachia. "I knew you would do the right thing. And Aina, do say hello to Aithne Oakforest for me."

The sky is blue as a robin's egg. Blue as only a summer's day can be. Blue as the eyes of her child.

Where is her child? He should be here. No, that was long ago. He's dead now.

Then why does she hear his voice?

Momma, *she hears.* Momma, *where are you?*

Here I am.

Then she sees him. The rotting corpse shuffling to her with outstretched arms. And she runs to embrace him.

15

"Well, that went pretty well, I thought," said Caimbeul.

We were sitting in the Dublin International Airport waiting for our flight to Tir Tairngire. Well, we weren't going directly to the Tir. I wanted to stop over in Austin and take care of a few things there first. Rubbing my eyes, I tried not to snap at him. How he could have thought things were going well was beyond me.

Oh, we were certainly given the royal treatment. But underneath I could feel the tension. The hostility. Things were changing and the Seelie Court knew it. They just didn't want to face what was happening. And he'd said barely a word the whole time.

But isn't that always the way of it? We hate change. Consider it the enemy. Yet it is the one constant in our lives.

I pushed an impatient hand through my hair, which had grown out just enough to be a nuisance. Sticking out every which way. Even in these dire times, I was vain enough to be concerned about my appearance. Or maybe it came from spending so much time alone with Caimbeul.

Had it really been almost two hundred years since we'd been together? I wondered at the thought that time could slip away so quickly. Why didn't I do something to stop it? I shook my head.

Stop what? Stop us from hurting each other? Stop us from being who we were?

"Something wrong?" Caimbeul asked.

"No," I replied. "Nothing much. I was just . . . remembering."

His eyes were bright and curious. *Oh, Caimbeul, you wicked creature to make me remember such things.*

"Paris?" he asked. "That café on the Rue Saint-Jacques . . . what was it called?"

"Well, Monsieur Rimbaud called it 'L'Académie d'Abomphe.' But I can't remember what it was really called."

He laughed. "I almost had a heart attack when I saw you there. You were wearing the most peculiar outfit . . ."

"It wasn't peculiar. It was the height of fashion.

Besides, I had to keep people more concerned with my dress than my nature. Unlike you, it hasn't always been easy for me to pass through human society. The color of my skin made it difficult at best. And my hair . . . I guess those are things people might remember."

"I remember," he said. His voice was soft, and suddenly it was as if we were all alone. That was a gift of his, making you feel as though you were the only person in the world. "The dress you wore was gray silk, shot through with jet beading. You had a hat on which had an enormous feather on it. Ostrich. Or was it peacock?"

"Peacock," I said softly.

"And you were drinking absinthe. I remember it looked as though you were embracing a lover when you drank."

I shut my eyes . . .

The first clear day of April. Paris, 1854. I sat in a café on the Rue Saint-Jacques. At the time, I didn't know its name. After a while, I wouldn't care. I had found something powerful enough to distract me from the horrors of living: absinthe.

My own sweet mistress. My dearest friend. The green fairy in the bottle who would steal a little bit of my mind every day. And how I adored it.

The rituals I'd built up. First, a stop at the bank where my pounds would be converted into francs. Then on to the small bakery for a pastry before I went to my first real appointment of the day. I told myself that as long as I ate something before I drank

I was fine. Hence the obligatory croissant, most of which I threw away on my way to meet my little friend.

That's what I called it: *ma petite amie.* Perhaps I should have said *mon amour,* for that was indeed what it had become: my dearest friend, my closest confidant, my love. And, just like all lovers, we had our rituals.

There were a number of cafés that sold absinthe, and I was well-known at all of them. In the spring and summer, I would settle myself at one of the outer tables. To take the air, of course. The air was very important—far more healthy than the smoky atmosphere indoors. In the winter, well, I just endured the smoke and noise. The things you will go through for a loved one.

After I sat at a table, a waiter would come over with the jade bottle, a water jug, and a glass. He would line them up neatly in front of me, then fill the glass with water. I tipped generously, and they knew what I wanted.

From inside my reticule, I would pull my silver absinthe spoon. It was slotted and diamond-shaped, intricately carved with flowers and scrolls. The spoon was placed over the glass. Plucking a sugar cube from the jar on the table, I would place it neatly atop the spoon.

Next came the moment I liked the best. First, I uncorked the bottle. The aroma of the absinthe floated to me. Licorice-scented and bitter.

Then I slowly poured the absinthe over the sugar. It dripped through the spoon into the water, swirling the color of new leaves, turning the water cloudy like a stormy day. The sugar cube sometimes wouldn't completely dissolve, and I would take it into my mouth, sucking my first bit of ecstasy from it.

When it crumbled into nothing, I would take the spoon from the glass, then slowly lift the glass to my lips. *What wonders will it show me this day?* I would think. *What sweet remembrances from the past would come to me? What memories would be created to fill my mind and keep me from the truth?*

And as I felt the warmth rush through my veins—sliding into my mind, seducing my thoughts—I would smile. Sometimes men would come to me and tell me how beautiful my smile was. So I would smile at them until they became nervous and went away.

And so, on that clear spring morning in April, when I saw Caimbeul for the first time in many a century, I thought, at first, that he was a product of my imagination. That I had conjured him up from the pretty places I went in my mind.

"Hello, Aina," he said.

I smiled. He smiled back. I didn't say anything; neither did he.

He didn't go away.

"I suppose it really is you," I said at last.

"I'm wounded," he said as he touched his chest over his heart. "Have you forgotten me so easily?"

I poured more water into my glass and put the spoon on top.

Sugar cube.

Absinthe.

"No," I replied. "Not so easily. Would you care for some?"

He took his pocket watch out of his waistcoat and opened it with a little click.

"Isn't it a bit early for this sort of thing?" he asked. "I hadn't figured you for the type."

The sugar cube crumbled in my mouth. My tongue was already numb and felt a bit grainy. Wonderful numbness.

"What type is that?" I asked. "The type that indulges in pleasure? Think of it, Caimbeul. All the years and years stretching ahead of us. All the ones behind. And it doesn't mean anything. Nothing we do matters. It all keeps happening again and again. I've spent plenty of time worrying about what has happened. And far too much concerned with what will happen. So, now, I don't care.

"This"—I raised my glass—"gives me a brief taste of happiness. I have had far too little of that."

Silently, I toasted him, then drank. Ah, nectar. I was borne up by angels into clouds of gossamer and silk.

He said nothing then. Just sat down there with me as I drank, then walked me home as the sun sank full and red into the gray twilight.

Every day he came and sat with me as I drank. Sometimes, I would go to a different café, but he always managed to find me.

One day I woke and discovered that I no longer wanted to go to the cafés. Caimbeul's presence had muddied the pleasure of the absinthe for me. I hated him for it. I dressed hurriedly, rushing out without my hat.

He was waiting for me at the café on the Rue Saint-Jacques.

"I hate you," I said.

"I know."

"You've ruined everything."

"Perhaps."

I stood there, frustrated, not knowing what else to say.

"Would you like to go for a walk?" he asked.

I narrowed my eyes. "Why?"

"Because it's a beautiful day," he replied. "And I'd like you to come with me."

I saw the waiter coming toward the table with the absinthe and water. My hands started shaking and I felt my mouth go dry. Caimbeul and I didn't say anything as the waiter put them on the table and left.

"Well," he said. "Are you coming?"

I looked at the absinthe. *Ma petite amie.* My life. *Just one more,* I thought.

I could feel my mouth pucker, anticipating the bite of the sugar, the anise bitterness of the absinthe.

Caimbeul held his hand out to me. Slowly, very slowly, I took it.

"Why did you stay?" I asked Caimbeul.

"When?"

"When you found me in Paris at that café. You could have left. It might have been better if you had. It was certainly out of character."

He looked out at the drizzling rain. The sky was

overcast and made the greens outside brilliant and a little surreal.

"I suppose it was the shock of seeing you there. You looked so . . . human. It surprised me. I had always thought of you as indestructable. No matter what knocked you down, you just kept getting back up. But there, in that place, you weren't ever going to get up again. I just couldn't stand to see the waste of it all."

The light from the fluorescents gave his skin a corpse-like pallor. It seemed almost incomprehensible to me that I had once held him in my arms. I felt like that had happened to a different person. A different Aina.

"Did I ever thank you?" I asked.

He turned toward me and smiled. The smile was crooked and made his face look lopsided. And I found it utterly endearing.

"Yes," he said. "You did."

"Good," I said.

And we sat there wrapped in our memories until the announcement came for our flight.

You have been hiding from me, Aina.

You must know there is nowhere you can run where I cannot find you.

No place that will afford you sanctuary.

I am coming.

Coming soon.

16

The international flight was cramped and exhausting. I jerked awake from another dream about Ysrthgrathe. He was in my mind again. Invading my thoughts and dreams just like he had all those years ago. It made me feel unclean. Like something slimy had crawled across my skin.

Caimbeul was asleep next to me. He snored a little and I gave him a bit of a push to make him stop. I wanted to wake him and tell him about my dream, but I didn't. I had learned long ago that it was better not to involve anyone else in matters concerning Ysrthgrathe.

Outside it was dark. I found flying to be strange, as though I were suspended in time and space. Another manifestation of my distrust of technology. Perhaps all this metal and cold, analytical thought reminded me too much of the Therans. The result of their devotion to purity had ruined so many. Like the Huns, they thought nothing of conquering and laying waste to any and all who opposed them. And like the Romans, they swallowed whole civilizations and digested them into unrecognizable pieces. They so believed in their own purity that they sacrificed the world.

But all of that time was gone. I had to stop letting it pull me into the past. What was important now was the future. I had to save it.

We landed in the Atlanta airport and made our connecting flight to Austin without any real delays. Oh, there's always some sort of drek that pops up when you enter the Confederated American States, but I still had a few connections of my own. A few hours later, we were catching a cab from Robert Mueller Airport to my sometime-residence in the western hills of Austin.

"I don't remember this place," said Caimbeul. He walked about the room pulling dust covers off the furniture and sneezing as dust flew up his nose.

The house smelled stale and I was opening windows. The clean, sweet scent of fall floated into the room. It was warm here, even in late October. I like that about Austin.

"I didn't come by it until nineteen thirty-four," I said. "As I recall, you were out of the picture by, oh, about fifty years."

"We did fall out of touch," he said. "I'm sorry about that."

"I'm not," I said. "We had said so many things by then. Things neither of us could take back. No, it was better that we got away from one another."

He opened the French doors leading to the balcony that wrapped around the front of the house overlooking the beginning of the Hill Country. Cedar and mesquite trees grew low and crippled by the fierce summers. It was as close to an alien landscape as I could imagine. Even now, when technology tried to cover every centimeter of earth, I believed that this land would reclaim itself if given half a chance.

"I like it here," he said. "It reminds me of another place—before . . ."

"Before the Enemy came," I finished. "Yes, it doesn't look the same, but it feels the same. Wild and untamed. There used to be more development here, but since the Awakening, it has gone back somewhat.

"After the Great Ghost Dance, the water spirits inhabiting the Barton Creek Watershed rose up and drowned a number of developers. They were having some kind of big ground-breaking on yet another big project. Apparently, the water spirits didn't like the idea, because they carried off the great-great-grandson of Jim Bob Moffett and several of his banker friends.

"There hasn't been much development since then, and the people who were living in property that was polluting the creek found themselves being tormented by water spirits. Most of them have left."

"Why are you still here?" Caimbeul asked.

"Professional courtesy."

We'd stopped for groceries on the way in, and after a quick meal of eggs and soylinks, we retired back to the balcony. Luckily, my freezer was still working and I had a supply of unground coffee beans laid in. We watched the brilliant red sun go down while sipping Kona blue and cognac.

"Why are we here?" Caimbeul asked. I had been waiting for him to get around to it, but I was surprised it took him so long. Perhaps he had gained some patience over the years.

"I wanted to get in touch with Thais," I said. "When last we spoke, he was in this area."

"Thais?"

"My child."

After I left Europe and Caimbeul's warm embrace, I came to America. I was achingly lonely for him, a fact that, in retrospect, seems rather foolish and trivial. But there it was. The rumors of the Great Ghost Dance had brought me here, or so I told myself. What I was really about was trying to forget Caimbeul and make something new out of my life.

I took a westbound train from New York to Saint Louis. Then I caught a stage to Sioux Falls. I knew Wovoka (he also used the Anglo name Jack Wilson, I recall) had convinced the Sioux that they had to use the great ritual magics to rid themselves of the whites and bring down retribution on their heads. He was right, of course, but wrong about the time.

The world wouldn't have enough magical energy in it for another hundred and thirty years.

But what concerned me was the news of his "visions." He claimed that God was sending him messages. I suspected there was another explanation, one I hated to consider: Thais.

I thought I'd stopped this passion of Thais's for popping up and causing mystical visions in magical-thinking cultures, but he was at it again. As I rode on the stage, my spine feeling as though it were being pounded through the ill-sprung seat and dust and dirt settling into everything I owned, I hoped I was early enough to put a stop to things before they blew out of hand.

By the time I reached Batesland, news was already making its way east about the massacre at Wounded Knee. I was too late.

It didn't stop me from looking for Thais. I knew I needed to rein him in again. How I hated the thought of another confrontation with him.

"I was wondering when you would come."

Thais.

He was hidden in the shadows of a low-hanging outcropping of rock. I wanted to see him, but, as if he knew that was my wish, he remained back in the darkness.

The wasted scenery of the Badlands spread out around me. It reminded me too much of how the world was after the Scourge. And to see Thais here, in this ruined place made me sad and angry at the same time. I'd told Thais that the world was not the

127

one he had grown accustomed to. That he must learn to change—but he rcfused.

My child.

Even after all these many centuries, I still worried about him. Wanted to know that he was safe. Would he ever forgive me for bringing him into a world that would never understand him?

"Hello, Thais," I said. "I see you've been busy."

Thais shrugged and looked a bit bewildered. "I don't understand," he said. "The magic should have worked." A frown crossed his face and I wanted to hold him and comfort him, but I knew that would not be allowed. It frightened me sometimes, how much he grew like his father.

"Magic isn't as powerful now," I said. "You know that. Why did you lead them to this destruction?"

"They loved me," Thais said. "It was just like in the old days. They looked at me and they didn't see a monster—they saw *me*. I was trying to help them. All they wanted was to have their land back. I could give that to them." He looked mournful. It made my heart ache. "I should have been able to give them that."

"Once," I said, "you might have. But no more. Those days are gone. Thais, you must stop this. I know what you've been doing. Those stone heads they dug up in the bed of the Trinity River. From the Pleistocene. I heard them described as obviously not human. My god, Thais, it was you. How could you have let them see you revealed?

"And what about Indochina? At least you tried to disguise your shape, but a seven-headed snake god?

I've told you that we aren't to interfere. There's too much at risk. What if they'd discovered what you really are? They might have killed you."

"I'm as hard to kill as my parents," he said, bitterly. "I am what you've made me. There is no place in this or any other world where I may live peacefully. Why did you make me?"

I looked away. Thais was right, of course. He never should have been born. But I was mad at the time. Out of my mind with remorse and grief. Selfish Aina.

"You must not do this again," I said. "It will only end in ruin. If not for you, then for your followers. Even now, when the magic is at a low ebb, you still, by your nature, have some power. Why don't you use it responsibly?"

"Oh, that's rich," he said, laughing harshly. Even so, it made me want to hold him and gaze into his eyes. Such power in my child. "You—talking about responsibility. You don't have the right."

"Mark my words, Thais. These tragedies will continue if you don't do something about it."

"What would you have me do, Mother? Exile myself to some mountaintop the way you did? Hide myself and live in isolation until the world is something else again? I need them and they need me. You cannot imagine how I feel when they look at me and love me. When they fall to their knees and beg for my blessing and I give it to them. I was born to be a god. To be adored and worshipped. You can't take that away from me."

"I'm not trying to take anything away from you . . ."

"You took my father away."

"Don't be a fool, Thais," I said. "That was an accident of birth."

He shrugged and looked away. I knew there was no use discussing this further. Thais had shut off from me, and nothing I could do or say would make any difference. How I wished that things could be different between us, but I knew I could as much wish for the moon for all the good it would do me.

And so we stood there, in that bare and barren place, divided by worlds and walls and the past that could never be undone.

She floats in a warm embrace. Hands touch her. Stroke her. Caress her until she trembles. Opening her eyes, she sees a faceless man. This doesn't frighten her—it's what she wants. To fall into the comfort of anonymity.

Safe and nameless.

17

"How are you going to contact Thais?" Caimbeul asked.

"A summoning," I said. "His nature is such that he won't be able to resist. I wish it hadn't come to this, but we haven't spoken in so many years. Since that terrible time after Wounded Knee."

"Why didn't you just call him up while we were in Tír na nÓg?"

"Too many enemies there," I said. "And Alachia doesn't know about Thais. At least not as far as I know. I would keep it that way. There are some things she should never know. And I want him to be on my ground. Not his; not someone else's."

A wave of exhaustion swept over me. Suddenly, I wanted nothing more than to go and sleep for the rest of my natural life. But I didn't have that choice. There was too much at stake.

I got up and walked back into the house.

Caimbeul drew the drapes as I turned off all but one light. Though it made little difference to my casting, I preferred less light. That way I could concentrate on what was happening with the spell rather than my surroundings.

"This would be a lot simpler if you let me help," said Caimbeul.

The edges of the room faded back into shadows. The few pieces of furniture still covered in sheets looked ghostly against the far walls. The night noises were muffled by the drapes. Occasionally, I could still hear the drone of a low-flying Lone Star Security chopper.

"Are you ready?" I asked. I wasn't sure which of us I was asking.

Caimbeul nodded and stepped back into the shadows. I knew if anything untoward happened, he would take care of me.

Taking a deep breath and closing my eyes, I let myself relax and block everything out but the spell I was about to perform.

I saw Thais in my mind. As he was when he was born, then later when I finally met him again. Grown up and changed into something so like me, and so like his father, that I wept until he made me stop with his voice and eyes.

That was Thais's gift, after all.

As I pictured him in my mind, I let myself slip

into astral space. There was the usual nauseating tug as I slipped between the veils. The ribbons flowed around me and into me until I couldn't tell the difference between them and myself. I was filled with the power. Exhilarating and fierce. This was what I was born to. I never doubted myself here. Here I knew who and what I was.

The veils parted as I remembered my task. I reached out my will, calling Thais to me. Commanding him to come to my summons.

Time passed interminably slow. Then sped to light.

I float then fall.

The universe is around me. Inside me. I am the universe: waiting and watching.

Across worlds I come. Through the blazing heat of a thousand suns. From the Void. Into the darkness.

From the darkness, I pull light.

My child.

Some things you cannot resist. The bond between a mother and child.

The brilliance of Thais blinds me as I pull him closer and closer.

Come to me, child.

And he cannot refuse.

Then we are falling. Falling through space and time. Back to earth.

"What do you want?"

Thais was standing in the center of the room. A

circle of blue energy surrounded him. I waved it away and he relaxed visibly.

"Was that really necessary?" he asked.

"Would you have come if I asked?"

He shook his head. "You abandoned me long ago. Why should I do you any favors now?"

I had hoped that old hurt had passed. But no, I was not to be forgiven any of my sins. Thais was still a child in so many ways. I had protected him too well.

"Very well, Thais, consider it a demand then," I said wearily. "I haven't the energy to fight with you about this now. There are other, more important, matters at hand."

Thais slid along the floor and pulled himself up onto the couch with his powerful arms. His thick, snake-like tail wrapped around his torso once, then hung down off the edge of his seat onto the floor.

"What does the Great and Powerful Aina want of me today? Perhaps I should go to the Wicked Witch of the West and retrieve her broom. Maybe I'll throw water on her and watch as she melts into brown sugar. Or there is always popping down a rabbit hole ... Which will it be?"

"Mind your manners, junior," said Caimbeul. "That's your mother you're addressing."

Both Thais and I turned toward him, open-mouthed. He shrugged.

"I think you've coddled him, Aina," said Caimbeul. "You've always protected him from ... the world."

"Coddled?" Thais said. "You call being born a

monster coddled? Look at me. Why did she make me? It was her selfishness . . ."

"Oh, grow up," snapped Caimbeul. "This isn't about you. . . ."

"Thank you," I interjected. "But why don't you let me get on with it?"

"Very well, but—"

I held my hand up and Caimbeul fell silent. A tight expression set on his face and I knew he was angry. It made me feel very warm inside.

I turned to Thais.

"Ysrthgrathe is back," I said.

Thais didn't say anything.

"Has he contacted you?" I asked.

"Why would I tell you if he had?" he asked.

"Thais, he's a liar. He spreads his misery that way. I know you want to believe . . . only the best."

"You don't know what I want," Thais said. "Why should I trust you more than him?"

"You know what he is," I said. "I've never kept that from you. There is more at stake here than your grudge against me. If he is back, then the world is at risk."

Thais rolled his eyes.

"It's always so dramatic with you, Mother," he said. His voice was that of a smirky, sarcastic fifteen-year-old. "How is it that you're always on hand to save the country, the planet, the universe? Don't you ever get tired?"

"Yes, Thais, I get very tired. I am *intensely* weary right now."

His tail twitched and tapped against the floor. The

scales that covered his skin were iridescent and gleamed in the low light. I wondered what happened when he had to shed his skin. So many little details about his life I didn't know.

"Very well," Thais said. "I'll tell you. He is here, on this plane. He contacted me a few days ago. But he didn't come to me in person—I had a dream. It was so vivid, unlike any other dream I've ever had.

"He explained . . . everything. He told me why you hated him. Told me the truth."

Caimbeul made an ugly noise and I looked over at him. A frown pulled at his mouth and he gave me a Why-the-frag-don't-you-just-shut-the-little-wackweed-up? look. I doubted he'd ever had children. I couldn't expect him to understand.

Thais had uncoiled himself from the couch and was slithering along the floor to the doors leading outside.

"Where are you going?" I asked.

"Outside for some fresh air," he replied.

I followed him. The temperature had dropped more than I expected. I rubbed my arms as goose-flesh broke out. We stayed there for a long time, wrapped in night sounds.

"Thais," I said at last. "I know I've been a disappointment to you. All those years apart, then later, when things turned bad for all of us. But . . ."

"Shut up," he said, turning violently toward me. "Just stop talking. How do you think I felt when he came to me? How could I deny him? You've cursed me with him."

He began to weep then. Terrible wracking sobs

that shook his frame. I wanted to go and embrace him, but I was afraid to. Afraid that he would reject me again. Oh, what agony it was to hear him in pain. I wondered how Caimbeul could resist the sound of it, for it tore me inside. Like I'd swallowed glass.

I forced myself to wait and watch until his tears began to dry and he seemed more in control of himself.

"Thais," I said. "I am so sorry. I never wanted you to have to face this. I tried to protect you."

"I know," he said. His voice was shaky and rough. "But you haven't been very good at that. Have you?"

And how could I answer that? But I suspect he didn't mean me to.

I don't know how long we stood there in the chilling night air. The stars frosted the sky in diamond-hard brightness. Then, later, I noticed that the black sky was turning purple-gray.

"What did he say?" I asked at last. I felt drained and exhausted. So empty that it didn't matter what he told me.

"He said you would come for me. He told me that you would try to stop him and it would do you no good." Thais's voice sounded weary. I wondered how I could help him, but then I realized there was nothing I could do for him now. That there are some things a parent cannot do for her child.

"Did he tell you if there were any other of the Enemy here?" I asked.

"No," Thais said. "But I didn't sense any others. I have always been sensitive to that sort of thing.

137

Your friend," he said, giving a jerk of his head toward the house. "He managed to stop something from happening a while ago. But the world has more than one point of entry. They are there waiting. Waiting for the moment when they can return."

"Did he say anything else?" I asked. "Anything at all might be important."

"Only that he's been waiting for you to come to him."

The sky was light now, moon hanging low against the horizon, looking strange and out of place so near the sunrise. We stood there in silence as the night fled from the day.

Aina sits before an old woman who has black witchy-hair and who wears gypsy colors. The air here is thick with incense and patchouli.

"Cut the cards," the woman says. Aina does so, feeling the coolness of the deck beneath her fingers.

The reading begins.

The cards lie face down—hidden and hiding their meanings. The first is turned up. The old woman gasps.

The Devil.

In a moment, he's crossed by the Moon and crowned by the Tower.

Aina shoves away from the table, unwilling to see what comes next.

"But you don't know how it ends," the old woman says.

"Why should I want to know?" Aina says. "After all, they're nothing but a pack of cards."

18

"You must send me back," Thais said.

We'd returned to the darkened interior of my living room shortly after sunrise. Thais was not fond of the light. He said it was too cruel.

"Why don't you stay here with me?" I asked. Caimbeul gave me a sharp look, which I ignored.

"I cannot," Thais said. "And you know why. But there is something I will tell you. Ysrthgrathe is not the only one of the Enemy here. There is another, just as subtle and as deadly."

"But where . . . how . . ."

"Deal with Ysrthgrathe first," Thais said.

I tried to get him to tell me more, but he refused. Finally, I had no other choice than to send him back.

The house seemed empty after Thais was gone. How I wanted to spend time with him. Get to know him. Figure out his peculiarities. But I had denied myself that long ago. And there was no going into the past to fix things.

We closed up the house again. Sheets covered the furniture. The alarms were set. I didn't look back as we drove away.

PART II

Millions long for immortality who do not know
what to do with themselves on
a rainy Sunday afternoon.

—Susan Ertz

She sleeps. And dreams. Safe happy dreams of times never lived and not imagined. They comfort her and calm her until she sinks. Sinks down into the long black darkness of her night.

19

Once, a human discovered what I was.

Like most curious men, he thought that the knowledge would gain him something. As though knowledge is a safe thing. Inert and powerless on its own.

It was 1998.

Fin de siècle fever was at an all-time high. There were riots and hysterical sightings of UFOs, messiahs, and dead celebrities. I'd bought my home in Scotland a few years earlier for an obscenely cheap price. An earldom, no less. Imagine, me a countess. It was to laugh.

I had settled into a smaller house on this property. The castle held no interest for me, being large and hard to maintain. I'd acquired quite a large fortune over my many eons. I could afford to take the, uh, long view on investments. There are some uses to being immortal—even if they're only financial.

It was from this vantage point that I was watching everything happening around me with great interest.

The signs were beginning. I knew it wouldn't be long before the magic returned.

So I began to gather together the things I would need to be prepared. For many centuries I'd hidden artifacts away, waiting for this time. It was on one such trip that I noticed him.

I'd just arrived from Scotland. The United States was still whole back then. The turmoil that would rip it apart was years away. Though I had spent many years in America over the last two centuries, I tried to stay away from the politics of the place. They seemed entirely too messy to me. But that's always been the nature of freedom.

As I ran to catch my connecting flight to New Orleans, I saw him. He was leaning against one of the pillars that lined the concourse in O'Hare. He wore a black T-shirt and faded blue jeans. A scuffed duffel bag lay at his feet like a lazy dog.

There was a look of intense concentration on his face, as though he were looking not at how I appeared, but at what was inside me. I didn't like it.

This was before the Awakening, and there was no way he could know what I really was for I'd found ways to disguise my true form. Oh, I appeared human, for the most part. My features were more delicate, perhaps, than most. And I was very thin. But my skin was as black as it ever was, and my hair was dark then, too. Some of the developments in the twenty-first century weren't all bad. I'd seen that blondes really don't have more fun, and I found that auburn really didn't suit me.

As I passed, the light reflected off his glasses, obscuring his eyes from me. I noticed that he had straw-colored hair sprinkled with a little gray. His beard was clipped neat and close, giving him an almost scholarly look. But then I could see his eyes again and once more I had the sensation of being looked through.

Frowning, I turned and hurried on down the corridor. I wouldn't have given him another thought, except that he boarded my plane not more than fifteen minutes later.

He was the last passenger on, probably flying stand-by. But why was he on this flight? And why had he been standing there in the corridor, as though he were waiting for me?

But he passed by me, not even making eye contact. What an imagination I had, I thought. The idea that he was following me. It was nothing. A chance meeting of the eyes, nothing more.

Despite the air conditioning, the air was hot and soupy. The smell of beignets hit me as I walked through the airport. One of the charms of the New Orleans airport was the immediate realization that this place was like none other in the United States. That Puritan priggishness was utterly cast aside here.

Maybe it was the weather, or perhaps the strong hold the French had placed upon the place centuries before, but here there was no hand-wringing over drinking, or gambling, or eating. In short, it was heaven, of a sort.

I caught a cab to the Fairmont Hotel, a gorgeous place with nine-meter-high ceilings in the foyer, crystal chandeliers, thick rugs, and the almost physical sensation of decadence. They also made the most fabulous pecan pie there. A southern confection that I've never liked anywhere else.

As the elevator was closing to take me up to my room, I thought I caught a glimpse of Black T-shirt through the milling hotel guests, but I knew it must be my imagination.

The French Quarter was a five-minute walk from the hotel. New York was the only other place in America where history butts up so closely with the present. I went down Chartres Street, then cut over to Royal. The heavy smell of the olive trees in bloom sweetened the air and almost masked the odor of the river.

Lined in antique shops and small art houses, Royal was my favorite street in the Vieux Carré. Bourbon may have been more famous, but the smell of vomit every few steps always put me off. There were some beautiful homes at the eastern end of Bourbon, but they hardly made up for the foul smells and lingering air of dissipation.

I slipped into one of the antique galleries: de Pouilly's. Over the years I'd made friends with the owners of many of these stores. They knew me as selective and willing to pay well for what I wanted. In return, I expected them to keep quiet about my visits and to let me ... wander ... in their shops. The whole Quarter was rabbit-warrened. You might enter an unpretentious storefront, only to discover a maze of rooms that led you through any number of connected buildings. I doubt there was anyone who knew all the twists and turns in these places.

A middle-aged man approached me as I entered. He gave off the superior air of someone who just knew I wasn't the sort who could afford to buy here.

"May I help you?" he asked in a tone that let me know in no uncertain terms that he thought he couldn't.

I picked up a bronze piece (not a very good reproduction at that) and turned it over as though considering.

"Tell Mr. Hyslop that Ms. Sluage is here," I said. I began fingering a porcelain bowl that looked to be an original Meissen. The clerk was obviously torn between telling me not to touch the pretties and trying to decide if I was, indeed, on speaking terms with his employer. Fear won out over officiousness, and he scuttled off like a cockroach.

A few minutes later (I was by now poking around in a large, intricately appointed armoire looking for secret doors), Mr. Hyslop appeared with the now very sweaty clerk in tow.

"Ms. Sluage," Mr. Hyslop said as he held out his hand. "It's so good to see you again. I trust you've been able to amuse yourself?"

As I backed out of the armoire and gave a little sneeze, Mr. Hyslop produced a handkerchief like a magician performing a trick.

"Bless you," he said as he pushed it into my hand. "I always get the sneezes when I start looking into these old pieces. No matter how hard we try to keep up, they seem to bring the dust with them."

"That's quite all right," I said, taking the proffered hanky. "I was just investigating to see if I might want this piece."

"Take your time, take your time," Hyslop said as he waved his clerk away. The clerk slunk off to go harass a couple who'd just stepped inside from the sweltering October air.

"What I'd like to do is take a look at those items you've been keeping for me, and make some arrangements for their transport."

Hyslop looked a bit concerned. "Are you not satisfied with our arrangement?" he asked. "I thought that—"

"No, no," I said, cutting him off. "It's nothing like that. I've just finally settled down in one place and I'd like to spend some time enjoying the things I've bought."

"Of course," he replied. "How foolish of me. Please, this way."

I followed him through the shop into a series of dimly lit twisting and turning hallways. Then up three flights of narrow stairs painted over so many times there were lumpy bumps like Braille on the railing and walls. It was very quiet here. You couldn't hear any of the usual street noise that bubbled through the Quarter day and night. He led me into his office, then fumbled around with his keys until he had the right one.

"Here we are," Hyslop said proudly as he flipped on the light switch.

The closet was small, but crammed to the top with arcana. Shelf after shelf with boxes labeled in a code we'd designed. One shelf held only boxes of books. Another, rare pottery. On yet another, articles of clothing. All had special significance. All were precious only to those who knew what to look for.

I could feel the pull of the energy in that little closet.

"I doubt anyone has a better collection of oddities," Hyslop said. "I just recently added this." He pulled a small box from one of the shelves and opened it. Inside was a long white veil, the kind women wore for their weddings and first communions. "It is rumored to have belonged to Marie Laveau's daughter."

"I didn't know she had one," I said. "A daughter, that is."

Hyslop nodded vigorously. "She kept her hidden away. She was afraid that when she died, the whites might kill her to keep the Voodoo under control."

"More than likely to keep the people under control," I said.

"That too, no doubt," Hyslop agreed.

"I'd like to look through these," I said, motioning to the closet.

"Of course," Hyslop said as he wiped his forehead with another clean white handkerchief. I wondered if he had a pocketful of them, magically pristine and freshly laundered.

"Alone," I said in a firm but kind voice. After all, I would need Hyslop and his unusual connections for some time to come.

"Of course," Hyslop said as he pocketed his handkerchief. "Just let me know when you're finished."

I smiled at him then, and he gave me a surprised smile back. I suppose I don't do that often. Smile, that is.

It took me the better part of the afternoon to go through the boxes. Most of the items were shams. The bones of some shamanistic practitioner, purported to have special curative powers. Shrunken heads, embalmed monkey remains, fossilized eggs. Books supposedly written in Crowley's own hand detailing his cabalistic findings.

I'd taken care to hide my most precious finds among these harmless trifles. They would be overlooked with all the other folderol. One hopelessly obscure book of cabalistic writings revealed complexities of such an esoteric nature that even I had trouble following it. The challenge of it excited me.

There were other items as well: suspicious bones, the source of which I knew only too well. How had they come to this place again? And so obviously long ago.

There was also a small painting depicting a creature I knew for a fact had not walked the face of this planet for at least seven thousand years. Yet here it was depicted in a piece that could not have been more than fifty years old.

I wrapped my treasures carefully and returned them to their innocuous hiding places.

I felt grimy and hungry all at once. It was almost five by Hyslop's grandfather clock. I pulled the chain to the light, then shut the closet door. It had an automatic lock, but I still jiggled the doorknob to see if it would open. It didn't.

On the whole, things were going well. I would have Hyslop crate everything up and ship it to my estate in Scotland. I'd already made the necessary arrangements with Customs, so there would be little delay in my receiving them once I was back home. I felt quite smug and pleased with myself and decided that I needed a decadent dinner to celebrate. I picked up the phone on Hyslop's desk and made a reservation for one at Antoine's for eight o'clock. I would feast tonight.

Walking back to the Fairmont, I noticed a van parked on a corner of one of the side streets I passed. It was painted dull black and had reflector stick-on numbers on the back window: 666. I glanced inside the van as I passed. A man, about forty-five or -six with a scraggly beard, sat in the passenger-side seat. He had a large potbelly barely covered by a faded-gray T-shirt. Around his neck he wore a pentagram. I had obviously just seen—Satan's Van.

Uh oh, I thought. *I better watch out because someone is going to come and carry me off in ... Satan's Van. The Armageddon starts tonight because—Satan's Van is in town. Oh, you better watch out, you better not cry, 'cause Satan's got his Van tonight. Satan's Van is coming to town.*

I really needed dinner.

Antoine's was unchanged. I'd been coming there for years whenever I was in New Orleans. I knew it was a bit touristy, but I couldn't help myself. They had the most marvelous Baked Alaska.

The elderly maître d' seated me at a small table in the front room. Like the rest of the buildings in the Quarter, Antoine's was made up of many rooms. People came through the front doors and disappeared like they were going down Alice's rabbit hole. There was even a hidden door or two in the place.

I'd just ordered and was admiring myself in the mirror over my table when I saw him. The black T-shirt from the airport. Only he wasn't wearing a black T-shirt now. He never would have been allowed inside in that. He wore a black jacket over a white shirt and muddy green tie. The jeans had been set aside for dark trousers.

I didn't take my eyes away from his image in the mirror as he talked to the maître d' for a moment, then walked toward me. I couldn't believe his brass.

"Dinner for one?" he asked. "That seems a lonely proposition."

"I like it," I said as I turned toward him. "And who the hell are you?"

"Ah," he said. "Well that's not as interesting as who the hell *you* are."

"Look," I said, beginning to get impatient. "I don't know anything about you except that I saw you at O'Hare—and now you pop up here acting as though you know me. I don't like mysteries or people who think they're being clever when in fact they're just annoying."

He pulled out a chair and sat down opposite me.

"You haven't been invited," I said, frowning. "Go away."

"Now, now," he said. His voice had the faint twinge of British lower-class to it. "Someone your age shouldn't get so excited. It might not be good for your health."

I looked around for the maître d', but he was talking to a new group who'd just arrived.

"I must say, you look awfully good for someone who's at least five hundred years old by my calculations."

He had my attention.

I looked at him carefully. He was working far too hard at being nonchalant. There was a telltale shine to his upper lip, and I could hear the dry click of his throat as he swallowed. Whatever he knew, it wasn't as much as he wanted to let on.

The waiter came with my soup. Vichyssoise. Thick and heavy with cream. He looked inquiringly at my new companion.

"Be so kind as to bring my friend here the same," I said. The waiter nodded and went away.

"What's that?" Black T-shirt asked.

"Vichyssoise," I replied.

He looked blank.

"Cold potato soup," I said.

He wrinkled his nose.

"Beggars can't be choosers and neither can you." I leaned back and studied him. This seemed to make him preening and nervous at the same time. "What's your name?"

"John Mortimer."

"And what precisely is it you want of me, Mr. Mortimer?"

He leaned forward, I resisted the urge to do so also. Habits die hard.

"I want to know the secret," he said. "I want to know how to be immortal."

"What on earth makes you think I'm immortal?" I asked.

He got a big grin. It was toothy and surprisingly sweet. I almost liked him for that smile.

"It started out by accident about four years ago," he began. "I was doing some research after reading an article in the newspaper." He pulled a small, yellowed newspaper clipping from his pocket. The headline read: Mystery Buyer Purchases Earldom for $700,000. I glanced over the article. It pretty much gave the dry facts of my acquisition of the Earldom of Arran. Everything except my identity, which I'd had them keep quiet.

"What has this to do with me?" I asked, handing the clipping back.

"You bought it," he said.

"And what makes you think that?"

"I like computers," he said. "I'm quite good with them. Every aspect. Programming, hardware—you name it. It's just this knack I have. Well, for some reason this article caught my attention. So I got on the Web and started trying to find out what I could about this mystery buyer. But pretty much everything after you bought the place was under deep wraps. Oh, I know all about the history of the place. That earldom was created in 1503 by King James IV.

The title is linked to the land instead of by blood. All that stuff. History is easy enough to find out.

"But about the new buyer—bloody nothing. That got me curious. Who would want so much privacy and why? So I started contacting other Net surfers in Scotland and eventually I came up with a few who knew all about the island. They were day workers hired to refurbish the house the new owner would be occupying.

"That's when I found out about you. It was quite a stir you being, well, not white. I even got along so well with my Scottish connection that they invited me for a visit. You were off on one of your mysterious trips. Everyone who worked for you always talked about your trips.

"So I went to visit my friends, and they showed me around the castle and the grounds. You've done a wonderful job keeping up the place. By the way."

I snorted and went back to eating my soup. The waiter came and placed a bowl in front of him. He frowned slightly at it, then took up his spoon and gave the soup a small taste. Apparently it was to his liking, for I got no more of his tale until he had finished the whole bowl.

"I never would have thought cold potato soup could taste so good," he said as he wiped his mouth.

"The things you learn every day," I murmured.

"So, as my hosts were showing me around, I began to notice a couple of things. There was all this old stuff around, but not all of it seemed to belong there, if you know what I mean. Not the usual rich collections of plates, clocks, and the like. No, your choices were so much more—peculiar.

"But the thing that got me most excited was this picture of you. A painting, I mean. Paul—that's the friend who I was staying with—had gone off to the bathroom and he left me alone in your study. There was a photo of you and some guy on your desk. Then noticed a stack of paintings against one wall. I flipped through them and came across this portrait.

"It was you. But it wasn't. I mean you looked just like you do now, only you were wearing some weird costume. Later, I learned it probably came from the Renaissance. I heard my friend in the hall and put the painting back. But, you know, that painting stayed with me."

"People have portraits done everyday," I said.

"But this one looked like hundreds of years old. The paint was dried and cracked. It *felt* old."

I rolled my eyes. "Oh, I didn't realize that among your many talents you are also an art historian. Let me see, you're a crack computer wiz, a clever defrauder of people's trust, and now you're an expert in dating paintings. What other talents do you have up your sleeve?" I asked.

His face flushed red, but he didn't answer me. The waiter came and took our dishes, then presented us with the paté. I broke off a bit of the French bread on the table and proceeded to smear a generous amount of my paté on it. I gestured to him to do likewise.

"Really," I said. "You must try your paté. It's marvelous."

"What is it?" he asked.

"Goose liver, butter, cognac, pepper, and cream, most likely," I said. "Do go on with your tale. It's so unusual to have such a fascinating dinner story."

He poked at the paté as if it would leap off the plate and attack him. Then he put the knife down. No guts, no glory.

"But see, the painting reminded me of another one I'd seen, in some class I'd had in school. So after I went to the library and started looking through books of artists . . ."

"Was this while you were still in Scotland?" I asked.

"Yes," he replied. "I was staying for a couple of weeks. Paul was glad to get me out of the house every now and again so he could have his girlfriend over. They were wanting to . . . well, you know."

"How touching."

"Anyway, I found the book I was looking for. It was on Rembrandt. It had all his paintings in it with little descriptions of what they were about and who owned them. But most of them are in museums. Except the one you have.

"But you obviously had all this money so I figured you could buy a Rembrandt if you wanted, but you couldn't have a portrait of yourself by him unless you'd been there."

"I hate to interrupt your psychotic ramblings," I said. "But haven't you ever heard of copycat painters?"

"Yeah, I heard about them when I was doing my research on you, but from what I came up with, that wasn't your style. You go for top-notch stuff if you bother with it at all."

"How flattering."

"Look, just stop trying to play like you don't know what I'm talking about. I've done research on you for the last four years. I know you've taken the identities of a number of other people. Graves are full of the babies whose names you've used. You've passed yourself off as your own granddaughter, as missing cousins. You're very good, I'll grant you that. But I have the documentation to back up everything I've found."

He pulled an envelope from his inside pocket and dropped it on the table. A sick feeling nestled in my stomach.

"Go ahead," he said. "Look inside."

Slowly, I wiped my fingers on my napkin. Moving slowly seemed to be a very good idea at the moment. I pulled the envelope to me and slid the contents out. There were letters from registry offices in several countries, copies of birth and death certificates, copies of land purchases in the names of some of the pseudonyms I've used. There was even a photo of the Rembrandt.

"How did you get this?" I asked holding up the photo. I was getting angry, but I didn't let him know. This was too terrible to let a foolish burst of temper out.

"Paul had to go back to your house for some repairs while I was there on my visit. I came along and snuck up to your study to make some shots."

"What do you want?" I asked. I felt sick. "Money?"

He shook his head furiously. "No," he said. "That's not it at all. I want what you have. I want to be immortal."

"And what makes you think I can make you so?"

"Because that's how it works," he said. "Like vampires, only I don't think you're a vampire. At least not the blood-sucking kind. You've got something and I want it. Why shouldn't I be like you? I figured out that you were immortal. I mean, shouldn't there be some kind of reward for that?"

I closed my eyes. Mortals. Humans. There were times when I thought Alachia's attitude toward them was dead on.

"And you think your reward should be that I make you into what I am?"

He smiled. "Yes, that's it exactly."

"Very well," I said. "Since you've asked so nicely."

I forced myself to choke down the rest of dinner. The lovely salmon, the delicate potato soufflé, the oysters, the escargot, even the marvelous Baked Alaska were all like ashes in my mouth.

John Mortimer was having no such problem with his meal. He attacked the food like a hungry dog. When he didn't recognize a dish, he would look toward me inquiringly and I would oblige with the information. Except with the escargot. I told him it was a rare kind of seafood, like oysters. Luckily, he

knew what oysters were. The one culinary achieve-
ment of his previous life.

That's how he referred to it: His Previous Life. As
though he'd already moved out of it and into a
greater place. He rambled on about the places he
would go, the things he would do, never once telling
me how he might acquire the means to achieve all
these tremendous feats. It had taken me centuries to
establish my own fortune. And still more time to attend to it. Money is like any other profession. You
had to look in on it, make sure no one else had decided they liked it better than you did and run off
with it. I found such things boring and loathsome in
the extreme. But I still had to do it. I just don't like
to talk about it.

". . . and then I thought you and I could . . ."

This jerked me back to my companion and his
ramblings.

"You and I could what?" I asked.

"Well, I mean, I thought that . . . I just assumed
that because you were going to make me like you
that we would be together. I mean until, you know,
whenever."

"Whenever what?"

"Whenever we got, you know, tired of each other.
Or until I was ready to be out on my own."

"I see, so not only am I to . . . convert you to your
immortality, but then I'm to be your nursemaid as
well?"

He blushed. "Not nursemaid, exactly, but, well
you know." He gave me quite a look then, and, had

I not been furious, I would have found it a bit interesting. But that was neither here nor there.

"So, I'm to become your um, paramour, shall we say, and make you immortal. And what exactly is it that I'm supposed to achieve from this equation?"

"What do you mean?"

"What I mean is, what's in it for me? Why should I make you, of all people, like me? Is it your charming personality? Or perhaps it's your wit? Maybe your sexual prowess? Come now, why should I bother with you?"

He was red again, but not from embarrassment. I think I might have offended him. What a pity.

"You'll do it because I'll expose you if you don't."

"Expose me to whom? The Agency in Charge of Finding and Keeping Immortals? Or maybe you'll go to the police. 'I beg your pardon, but there's a woman I know who's immortal.' They'll laugh you out of the office. Your whole story is preposterous. There won't be a dry seat in the house."

"All I have to do is make one phone call to the right sort of newspaper. They love this sort of thing. Only when they start digging, they'll find out it's true."

"They'll wet themselves laughing."

"Do you really want to risk it?"

The little maggot. I hadn't thought he had the brass for it.

"I thought not," he said. And smirked.

He really shouldn't have smirked.

* * *

I paid for dinner and we began walking through the Quarter. I didn't want to lead him straight toward the hotel, though I suspected he already knew where I was staying. What to do with him? I wondered. The crowd was thicker now that it was getting on toward nine o'clock. Mostly there were badly dressed tourists in too tight T-shirts with cute sayings on them. Some carried plastic cups with drinks in them. The smell of beer and sticky-sweet Hurricanes was overpowering.

I led us toward Chartres Street, then on toward the riverwalk. The smell of the Mississippi was heavy and thick like new-cut earth. It blended with the sweet aroma of the olive trees. For some reason it gave me a stab of hope, this strange combination of odors. It reminded me of another time and place. But such pleasant memories would get in my way now. I needed to attend to the matter at hand.

We walked past the homeless people who were sleeping in the park and stepped over the ones who had simply lain down where they were. Every few paces or so, we were approached by someone asking for money. Most of the panhandlers had a ready patter, some hard-luck story about why they needed just another dollar. I gave to them willingly. Life presented us with enough indignities in just the living of it, so why make it worse if you could help?

"Why are you giving them money?" hissed John. He glanced around as though he expected someone to jump up at him and demand money.

"Because I have it. They need it. And I don't

mind giving to them," I said. "Why do you care anyway? It isn't your money."

"You're just encouraging them," he said. "If no one gave them any money they'd have to get a job."

"Let me see if I understand you," I said. "You think these people prefer to live meaner than any animal. That they are so unwilling to work that they would rather sleep on the ground in the cold, go without food, beg coin from strangers in the most humiliating way possible, and live in filthy rags? That is, of course, assuming that they are mentally stable enough to hold work or even have such rudimentary skills as reading, writing, or arithmetic. How silly of me to be so completely fooled by their clever charade.

"Of course, I'm in the company of someone who wouldn't sully his hands with something as vulgar as say, extortion."

"You know, you can be a real bitch," he said.

I touched my hand to my heart. "I'm mortally wounded," I said.

We walked down by the river for a while, until the sidewalk petered out and there was a sudden lack of street lights. John looked nervous, but I knew there was nothing to worry about, yet.

"So you want to become immortal," I said. "What if I told you I can't do it? That this is something you're born with or not. That I can no more make you immortal than any stranger off the street could."

He frowned. "You're just trying to confuse me," he said. "You told me at the restaurant . . ."

"I told you that so you wouldn't make a scene. Even if I wanted to, I couldn't change you from what you are. I don't have that power. Why would I lie to you?"

"Is this a test?" he asked.

I groaned. "No, it is not. It's the truth."

"You just don't like me. That's why you're doing this. Well, it won't work. And it doesn't matter anyway. I figured out what you are, and that's worth something. Don't think you'll fool me the way you've fooled everyone else."

"Oh, no," I said. "I wouldn't dream of that." *I think you're a special kind of fool,* I thought. "You know, becoming immortal doesn't just happen overnight. It takes a while for the process to work."

"But you can start it soon, can't you?"

"Oh, yes," I said. "But first, I must make some preparations." I tossed him the key to my hotel room. "I'm in room 1650 at the Fairmont. I'll be back before midnight."

"I'll be waiting," he said.

I didn't say anything, just turned and went back toward the Quarter.

I knocked on the door of my room at 11:45. The vid inside was loud enough for me to hear it through the door. Then the door swung open. I had half-hoped Mortimer might realize how foolish this whole thing was, but no, there he was, sans jacket, and barefoot.

"Glad to see you've made yourself comfortable," I said.

"Yeah, well, given the circumstances, I didn't think you'd mind."

"Push that bed up against the wall," I said. As he did so, I also pushed every other piece of furniture in the room against the walls, making a nice-sized space in the center of the room.

"We're going to do it here?" he asked.

"Why not?" I asked. "This place has always had a great deal of magical energy. Besides, this is just the start of the process, and I know how anxious you are to embark on your new life."

"Yeah, well, I guess I thought I'd have more time."

"Time for what?"

"I don't know," he replied. "To say goodbye."

"You can't say goodbye, but you can go back and make some preparations," I said. "I'll explain everything after the ceremony."

I crouched down and poured out the contents of the bag I'd brought back with me. Luckily, Marie Laveau's House of Voodoo had just the sort of things that would help in my little charade. Candles, skulls, charms, unidentifiable bones, incense, and assorted effluvia tumbled onto the carpet. Feathers I'd picked up in the park came from my jacket pocket.

I shoved everything to one side. "Stand here," I instructed, pointing to the center of the room. I placed the candles around him in a rough circle, then lit them. The incense I lit and stuck in-between the drawers of the bureau. Then I switched off the lights and went over to the window and drew the drapes.

The effect was getting pretty good. Lots of sandal-wood smoke wafting through flickering candle light. I made him hold out his hands and dropped a skull into one and the strange bones into the other. Then I made him open his mouth and popped one of the charms inside. I almost started laughing at the face he made, but I knew that would break the spell.

The rest of the charms I placed in his pockets and down his shirt. Then I began to chant softly and wave my arms in front of him. In Sanskrit I told him what a complete imbecile he was and how his mother was probably a goat-herder who slept in cow dung for fun while she mated with snakes at the bottom of a cesspool.

From the expression on John Mortimer's face, I knew he thought he was being transported to the next level of existence. And how close he was.

It took me a while to run through his entire family lineage back to his great-great-grandparents, but I managed to think up appropriate comments for all of them. Now it was time for the big finish. I distracted him as I tossed flash paper into one candle after another. He gave a little squeal and jumped.

"Ack," he said. "I've swallowed the charm."

"That's all right, you're supposed to," I said. "How do you feel?"

He looked down at himself as though he expected to see something different.

"The same. I'm getting a bit of a headache from all the incense," he said. "Are you sure it worked?"

"Oh, I almost forgot," I said. "The most important thing."

I leaned forward and pressed a kiss to his forehead. I held it there for a long time. I could see the weave of his life. Could feel the singsong of his blood as it raced through his veins. His delicate and vulnerable veins. Especially those in his brain. So thin. So easily stressed. It took a bit out of me, the subtlety of it, but I had no other choice.

He stepped back from me.

"What's this?" he asked, reaching out and touching my cheek.

There, suspended on the tip of his finger, was a single blood tear.

"The price of immortality," I said.

"I think I felt something," he said.

"I'm sure you did." I reached out and gently wiped the tear away.

The aneurysm killed him on his flight back to London. I had told him to go home and get his belongings and meet me in Scotland. It being a slow news day, his death actually made the paper in a small item. Freak accident, the report said. A terrible tragedy for one so young.

November 21, 1998

Anna Sluage
Earldom of Arran
Arran Island, Scotland

Dear Countess,

It is my most embarrassing duty to tell you that my late client, one John Mortimer, had apparently become fixated on you during the last few years of his life. Upon his death, I was instructed to open a parcel he'd left with me a few months ago. In this parcel were documents and writings of Mr. Mortimer claiming a tale as regards you, of the most fantastic sort. His instructions to me, as his solicitor, were that should he die under unusual circumstances I was to go to the media with this story.

Due to the nature of my client's death, I recognized these bizarre accusations as the demented ravings of a mentally ill man. It is a great sadness to his family that they did not realize how ill he was until his untimely demise.

Please rest assured that I have forwarded all these materials to you for you to dispose of as you will. No copies have been made by me or my office. I can only hope that my client did not make himself a burden on you. Rest assured that this matter will go no further.

Sincerely yours,
Mecham Bernard, Esq.

Several months later I received a note from John Mortimer's mother. She had gone to clean out his flat and had discovered his diary and a bulletin board covered with photos of me. In her letter, she said that she hoped her son had not bothered me. She explained that his obsession with me was no doubt caused by the same weakness in his brain that killed him.

She also told me that she had destroyed all the papers and pictures of me she had found.

I wrote her back, thanking her for her concern, and assured her that her son had never bothered me in the slightest. We actually developed a bit of a correspondence, which lasted until her death in 2021.

She's traveling in a car. Or maybe it's a bus. She isn't sure, because it continually shifts shape and form. Caimbeul is driving. He is wearing that horrible makeup. Garish and clownlike. A hideous red gash of a mouth. Black diamonds over his eyes. Hair streaked with blond and orange. His usual garb is replaced with faded blue jeans, cowboy boots run down at the heels, and a washed-out T-shirt that says: Ninety percent of everything is drek.

"I was wondering when you'd get here," Caimbeul says.

"Where is here?" she asks.

"You know," he replies. "It's wherever you want it to be."

She glances out the window, which shows an endless display of black night. The headlights occasionally catch a scrubby tree, then slide back over the broken road. Looking back at Caimbeul, she sees that the saying on the shirt has changed: I prefer the wicked to the foolish. The wicked sometimes rest.

"Didn't? Wasn't?" she asks.

"Oh," Caimbeul says looking down at his shirt and shrugging. "It's your dream. Don't ask me. I'm just along for the ride."

"You always did steal your best lines," she says.

He drops the car into overdrive. It surges ahead, the G-force slamming both of them back in their seats.

"Hang on," he shouts over the roar of the engine. "It's going to be a bumpy night."

20

Runner's Revenge was blasting a cover of the old tune "Do You Believe in Magic?" over the trideo system at LAX. They'd done something strange to the song, pumping a reggae beat under the glass-shattering shriek of the cyberjacked vocals of the lead singer, whose species, much less gender, I had yet to determine.

As the lead singer seemed to pop from the trideo, I looked around for connecting flight info. Nothing as simple as a screen showing takeoffs and departures, I thought. Just as I was about to get on a tear about the uselessness of technology without practicality, Caimbeul grabbed me by the arm and steered me to a bank of flatscreens on the opposite side of the trideos.

We had ten minutes to make our connection to Portland on Cinanestial. Wasn't that always the way of it, though?

"We'll never get through Tir customs in time," I said. "When's the next flight out?"

Caimbeul grabbed my bag and slung it over his shoulder.

"Oh ye of little faith," he said. "While you were puttering about with Thais, I was making a few calls. No need to tell me how much you appreciate

171

it. Let's just say we'll be experiencing no trouble about our VAVs. And, most importantly, there will be no need for your strong-arm tactics. Now, don't give me that look."

"I'm not giving you a look," I said as I raced along beside him. Though I am long-legged, I had to break into a quick trot to keep up with him. After all, he is a good head taller than me.

"I knew you'd never give up a tissue sample, and you know how persistent these low-level customs security types are. I didn't want you to do to them what you did to our friend in the UK."

"It got us in, didn't it?"

"But here it might set off alarms. And I want our arrival to be as quiet as possible. I've arranged things with a friend. We should have no problems."

I frowned. "And who are we going to be beholden to for this favor?" I asked. "I don't like owing anyone anything if I can help it. This will be dicey enough. You know what the politics are like here. They make the Borgias look like a close and friendly family."

"I'm the one with the favor owed, not you," he said. He sounded a bit exasperated. "I had forgotten how difficult you can be on a trip. At least you've learned to pack a little lighter."

"And just what is that supposed to mean?" I said. But it came out more like, "And . . . just (gasp) what . . . isthatsupposedtomean?"

"Nothing," he said. "Do you have your Visitor's Authorization Visa ready?"

"Yes," I said. "And don't change the subject. I

don't recall you ever complaining about my luggage before. Have you been nursing this grudge for long? As I recall, the last time we traveled together for any length of time was back in eighteen ninety-eight. Vienna. And everyone had trunks, not just me. You had two of them. Plus a rather large leather portmanteau that never would have fit on any horse ..."

"We're here," he said.

I slid to a stop. The sleek silver, green, and white of the Cinanestial counter was in front of us. A male elf stood at the counter with a datacord jacked into a silver slot in his left temple running to the 'puter hidden behind the top of the counter. At the door to the plane stood another elf, who looked pleasant enough until you noticed that she had cyberware implants in both arms and a nasty-looking taser slipped into a tasteful sleeve on the side of her uniform.

Both elves were wearing the Cinanestial uniform: skin-tight dark-green material with bold color blocks of silver and white. Though I suspected they were both expert at being polite and serving the passengers, anyone who gave them any grief would likely be pulling pieces of his favorite anatomy part from his throat for a long time to come.

Before we even reached the counter, another uniformed elf appeared in front of us. I didn't see where she came from, and the fact that she got the drop on me irritated me to no end.

"I need to see your VAVs, please," she said. The please was a mere formality. I had spent most of my time avoiding Tir Tairngire—and with good reason. Now I was waltzing in chin-first. Even with

173

Caimbeul as my companion, I wondered if this wasn't a bigger mistake than facing Ysrthgrathe alone.

I passed my VAV across to Caimbeul, who put it with his and gave it to her.

"Stay here," she said. She turned and walked over to the elf at the desk. They talked together in low voices for a moment, then the counter-elf said something to the one with our passports. The customs elf put a deliberately blank expression on her face, then walked back to us.

"Go on through," she said. "Have a good flight."

Caimbeul took our papers and walked past without saying a word to her. I followed, trying hard not to give a smug grin. I failed. Oh, well.

Just as we reached the door to the loading ramp, I heard a commotion behind us. I looked over my shoulder in time to see the customs elf tossing a scared-looking troll to the floor as if he were a ragdoll.

All brawn, no brains. Some things never change.

The flight to Portland was about two and a half hours. I didn't make small talk with Caimbeul. I was afraid I might blurt out that he'd been in my dream, and then I'd have to listen to him crow about that for the rest of the flight.

He was a conceited bastard under the best of situations—I didn't want to think about how obnoxious he would become if I told him.

And what was going on with my dreams anyway? I hadn't dreamed of Ysrthgrathe in several nights. It scared me because if he wasn't coming to me through that window, where was he going to come from?

Was he already here and waiting for me? Waiting to rip my life apart again? Or had I just dreamed him up? Pulled him from my nightmare past as surely as I had pulled him to me all those millennia ago? I wasn't sure now. No, I had to be sure. The fate of the world was riding on me. There was no room for mistakes.

We sank into the gray clouds as we made our approach to Portland. From up in the golden sky to down into the rain and muck. I could barely make out the green land below as we popped in and out of the clouds. Rain smeared the double-paned windows.

"How are we going to get the Council to hear us?" I asked.

"I'm going to petition the High Prince," he replied.

"Lugh Surehand?" I asked. "I didn't realize you were on such close terms."

Caimbeul looked away.

"Don't tell me," I said. "He has no idea that we're coming, does he?"

"I'm sure he knows we're coming. There's very little that goes on in Tir Tairngire that he doesn't know. But I haven't contacted him directly. I thought it would be better to wait until we're actually in Portland."

"Why? And stop fidgeting."

"I'm not fidgeting. I don't fidget. That's an awful word. Fidget. You make me sound like a three-year-old."

"If the age fits."

He ran a hand through his hair, dislodging the band that held his ponytail. Then he cursed when the band got tangled up in his hair. The more he tugged at it, the worse the snarl became. I slapped his hand away and gently began to work it loose.

"It's Aithne, isn't it?" I asked. "You're worried that when Aithne knows I'm in Portland, he'll do everything he can to see that I'm not heard."

I was surprised to see him look so embarrassed. The band came loose and I ran my fingers through Caimbeul's hair to make sure there weren't any more tangles. It was as silky as I remembered, cool on top and warm near the nape of his neck. It was an odd moment, filled with promise and regret. Then I pulled my hands away and held out the band to him. His fingers slid over mine as he took it, and lingered there for a moment.

"It's been so long, and he still hasn't forgiven me," I said. "I know I have no right to expect that he would, but all the same there's the hope in me that he might."

Caimbeul took my hand and gave it a little squeeze. "He attends his grudges like a jealous wife. Age hasn't tempered him. It's only made him more of what he is. But isn't that the way it is with all of us?"

"I suppose. But what about you and Ehran? I know you engaged in the Game some time ago. Did

176

that resolve any of your differences? Or did it merely let you keep them simmering for another hundred years or so?"

"Simmering, my sweet, simmering always. I never like to bring things to a boil."

I held his hand tightly for a moment, then released it.

"I seem to remember a time or two when that wasn't the case."

"You are an evil woman, Aina."

I just smiled at him, then went back to looking out the window.

We passed through Tir customs easily. Whatever mojo Caimbeul had worked with his friend, it breezed us through the usual tediousness of the bureaucracy. I'd made it a point in the past to avoid Tir Tairngire at all costs. Oh, I'd been here a few times, but always as quickly and discreetly as possible. Though I knew Aithne would never act against me directly, I wasn't about to force the issue.

Tir Tairngire was, after all, his baby.

He'd cooked the idea up with Sean Laverty, Lugh Surehand, and Ehran. They'd moved with a purpose and precision to establish the Tir that preempted anyone who might have stood in their way. Not that I would have been foolish enough to try. I like to think that I've developed some measure of sense in my old age.

They tricked the Salish-Shidhe Council into giving over part of their land to the elves. Oh, I had to admire their cunning. Like all good mundane magic, it was done with clever distractions and sleight of hand.

It was Ehran who did the initial dirty work. And how he must have enjoyed the charade—posing as an Amerindian—Walter Bright Water—newly released from the Pyramid Lake Re-Education Center. He pretended that his wife and children had died there, then deceived the tribal elders with his knowledge of Cascade Crow tribal rituals. The treachery of it astounds.

Perhaps I am letting my history with Caimbeul color my comments, for his and Ehran's relationship is a bitter one from long ago. The enemy of my friend is my enemy. Not that Ehran had the slightest idea of my opinion of him, of course. That would be foolishness of the first water.

Anyway, eventually, he received a place on the S-S Council, and parlayed that into his final plan. He encouraged the segregation of metahumans, saying that Awakened individuals were better off away from humanity and their prejudices. But, at the same time, he encouraged the Salish-Shidhe and the other Native American Nations to welcome metahumans into their territories.

This brought metahumans into NAN and the Salish-Shidhe territories in ever-increasing numbers over the years just before the establishment of the Tir. Before Bright Water disappeared (faking his death, by the way. Something I know he is quite proficient at), he encouraged the metahuman population to segregate itself into the southern region of the Amerindian territories. They did so, and this was the beginning of what would later become Tir Tairngire.

Of course, Aithne and the others hadn't been sitting by doing nothing, but they did let Ehran have all the fun. After "Walter Bright Water's" death, they appeared on the scene and began to lead the "renaissance in the south." By the time there was a formal declaration of independence by the Tir, the Salish-Shidhe was no longer a cohesive power and there was nothing NAN or any other nation could do to stop them.

By this time, of course, Ehran had re-emerged as himself. The rest, as they say, is history. The Tir went on to be recognized by every other nation, with the notable exception of Aztlan. But then they are both special cases unto themselves.

Now they had set themselves up as Princes, no less. Of course, that is how most of us thought of ourselves. After all, we had always ruled, whether overtly or covertly. The hand that guides the puppets does not have to seen.

They had made all the preparations, but I suspected they still didn't believe the time would come when they would have to use them. Only that they would have the world made over in their image and no one would stop them.

None but those who had always stopped us before.

Caimbeul had booked us into the best hotel in Portland. It overlooked the Willamette River and was as lush and palatial as any Louis the XIV wet dream. I'd never been particularly impressed by the elven fondness for royal pomp and circumstance. It seemed pretentious and ultimately destructive to me. But then no one had asked my opinion on the matter, had they?

I wasn't sure what influence Caimbeul wielded here, but there was enough bowing and scraping to make even Alachia happy. We were shown to the uppermost penthouse, being informed along the way that the High Prince had resided here while having his home remodeled.

Caimbeul and I were suitably blasé about the whole situation. And why not? We'd seen Versailles at its height. And the Taj, that jewel of a building, small yet almost perfect. How could any hotel room, no matter how sumptuous, compare?

Finally, we were left alone. The staff would have to be spoken to about the hovering. I dropped down onto one of the brocade sofas, sinking into the real feather cushions.

"Well, what now?" I asked. "How long do you think we have until Aithne finds out I'm here?"

Caimbeul went to the French doors leading out to the terrace and pushed them open. The air was sweet up here, with none of the sour, acrid smells I normally associated with cities. I knew they'd done much to manipulate the land in the Tir. The magical energy fairly pulsed in the air. If they'd put out a large neon sign telling the Enemy "Come and get us," they couldn't have done better.

I knew there were now old-growth forests where

only a few years before there had been fallow land. Extinct species populated these forests—how they'd managed that I suspected I knew, but I hoped I was just being paranoid.

"Not long," Caimbeul said. "Aithne has spies everywhere. Fortunately, he's away from Portland right now. And we know Alachia was in Tír na nÓg. Though I suspect after our visit she might be here already. But I've never been very good at predicting what she will do next.

"There's a celebration planned for this evening. Something to do with The Rite of Progression."

I got up from the couch and came over to where Caimbeul stood by the open doors. It was already getting dark. The gray misting sky oppressive and bleak.

"You don't like it here," I said.

"No."

"Neither do I. It reminds me too much of the days when Alachia was Queen. What she turned so many of us into. It frightens me because I think it could all happen again. Especially when I see that the Enemy is coming again."

Caimbeul stepped behind me, then wrapped his arms about my waist. It was very comforting to stand there in the slowly falling chill night with him warm and solid against my back. He rested his chin on my head.

"But things are different now," he said. "The world is different. We can keep the past from happening again."

"I hope you're right."

"I am," he said. "I am."

And we stayed there for a while, in the darkness, resting against each other for support.

"Did you think I had forgotten you?" Ysrthgrathe asks.

She freezes, finding herself not in the safety of Caimbeul's arms, but embraced by her enemy. His arms are thickly muscled and hold her so tight that even though she struggles, it's as if she has never moved.

Then his mouth is at her ear, breath hot against the tender flesh. "I have been waiting for you so patiently, my sweet. This delay is but a heartbeat for me. The blink of an eye. And there is nothing you can do that will stop me this time. Not running to your precious Aithne. Not dragging that clown behind you. None of them will save you from me this time."

Somehow, she manages to slip free of his grasp, but then he laughs and she knows he's let her go.

"This isn't the past, Ysrthgrathe," she says. "I'm not that foolish girl anymore. You can't frighten me like you did then."

"Liar," he says.

21

Caimbeul had insisted we bring formal attire. I had wondered at this, but as we entered the grounds of

Royal Hill where Lugh Surehand occupied the Royal Palace, I was glad of his foresight. An elf attired in livery opened the door to our limo.

I'd also wondered at Caimbeul's choice of vehicle until I saw the battery of armaments, assault weapon controls, and other trinkets loaded onto the seemingly innocuous luxury car. The driver was a nasty-looking troll who seemed to know Caimbeul. Or at least they exchanged those knowing sort of nods that men think are very casual but anyone with half a brain can see right through.

I wasn't sure whose Rite this celebration was for, but Surehand had gone all out. There were white tents scattered across the manicured lawns. Pathways between the tents were lit by magical means—nothing so mundane as electric lights for Lugh Surehand's guests. Garlands of flowers were draped over anything that stood still. Staff dressed in Surehand's colors circulated among the guests carrying tray after tray of wine and Epicurean delights. Even the weather had been manipulated. It was cool but not chilly, and the rain that had plagued us all day was finally gone.

I noticed that all the servants seemed to be orks and dwarfs and almost all the guests elves. I knew that when the Tir was established they'd made a big show of inviting non-elven metahumans, but I suspected that it was more the desire for cheap labor than altruism.

Hanging back at the edge of the party, I stayed in the shadows, pulling Caimbeul with me.

"What are they?" I hissed, pointing at several

elves dressed in solid-black partial body armor that resembled the plate mail worn by knights in the thirteenth century. Some sported SMGs, others more lethal-looking weapons. Around them I could discern magical auras.

"They're Paladins," he replied. "Part of Surehand's personal guard. He takes younger sons from the noble families and makes them swear fealty to him. Ehran started the whole thing, I think.

"It keeps them out of trouble. Otherwise they'd be brawling among themselves, or plotting to do in their older siblings. Let's face it, this hierarchical society they've reinstated has some serious drawbacks."

I nodded. "Only so many can be on top, and since who ends up there is already decided, it leaves everyone else with any ambition pretty much hosed. It's actually a pretty clever solution. Channel all that brawn and energy into supporting the status quo.

"But why would Surehand need them here? I know he has some sort of magical wards to protect this place. And I'm sure there's a mundane security system in place. Is there really that much chance for assassination?"

Caimbeul shrugged. "Probably not, but would you want your bully boys to think they're being shirked socially? Much better to keep them handy."

"And you wonder why I've never been much for society," I said. "This all seems like such a waste of time to me. I don't have the stomach for it."

Caimbeul reached out and placed his hand lightly on the small of my back. I was wearing a gown cut very low in the back. The contact of his hand against my naked flesh made me shiver.

"I think we'd best make ourselves known," Caimbeul said. "I wouldn't want to get caught lurking here in the shadows."

We moved forward then, stepping into the golden wash provided by the floating wisps of light. Caimbeul guided us from one group to the next with the practiced grace and smoothness I'd forgotten he possessed. After all, he'd spent time both in Alachia's court as well as the courts of the Northern Kingdoms, while I had made myself an outcast from society many times over.

With each group, we moved closer and closer to Lugh Surehand. It was a ballet of conversation, compliments, and jockeying for position. I was so caught up in admiring Caimbeul's easy skills as a courtier that I forgot for a moment to pay attention to who was moving toward *us.*

"Aina," came a deep voice to my left. "It has been far too long. How are you, my dear?"

I found myself being kissed on both cheeks by a tallish man dressed in an exquisitely cut suit of black worsted wool. His long, steel-colored hair hung unbound down to the middle of his back, and he had almond-shaped, preternaturally golden eyes.

"Oh come now, Aina. Don't you recognize me?"

I blinked, taken aback by the unexpected intimacy. Then I looked more closely at him. "Lofwyr," I said. "I didn't expect to see you in such a place. Nor in this guise."

The dragon laughed. "When in Rome and all

that," he said. "But what about you? Sheep's clothing? Or is it a new designer? As I recall, you were more fond of Chanel than anything else. But this doesn't look like anything I've seen lately."

I smoothed a hand over the gray velvet of my dress, a nervous gesture that I caught and made myself stop.

"I had no idea you were so interested in fashion," I said. "A new hobby, or are you just bored?"

"Nothing is boring for long here," he said. "And now you have appeared after such a long time. Have you come to be reunited with your people?"

I gave him an incredulous look. "I believe my position on 'my people' was made long ago, Lofwyr. And you'd best not forget it. It makes my task here all the more difficult."

"So, you have come to play Cassandra," Lofwyr said. "You'd do well to remember what happened to her."

I took a drink of my champagne to keep from frowning at him. At least it was Krystal and not a bad vintage. The privileges of power. Caimbeul had listened to our conversation without saying anything. I glanced at him to judge his mood, but he was looking past Lofwyr. I turned, following his gaze, and saw that a young man was staring at us.

I froze, for a moment thinking that I was seeing Aithne Oakforest, but this elf was too young to be Aithne. On second glance I saw the differences between them. The slightly petulant mouth. The spoiled expression on his face. The bored gaze. He had some of his father's coloring and bone structure, but the hair was too light and the eyes darker. Still, there was no doubt in my mind that this was Glasgian, Aithne's oldest son. Or at least the oldest surviving one.

The thought of Aithne's son pushed the breath from me. That I could still feel the pain of this moment, even after all this time, astounded me. And I knew that my hopes for Aithne's forgiveness were in vain.

I felt Caimbeul's hand on my elbow and heard his voice in my ear as though it were coming from a long way off, like an old-fashioned radio broadcast. "I know seeing him is a bit of a shock, Aina," Caimbeul said. "But don't let it throw you. He isn't Aithne, and he's not the ghost of Hebhel come back to haunt you. Remember what's important now."

I turned toward Caimbeul, pulling my gaze from Glasgian. "I'm sorry," I said. My voice was reedy and thin in my ears. "He gave me such a start."

"Are you all right, Aina?" asked Lofwyr. "You look positively green. Maybe you should sit down."

"No," I said, more firmly this time. "I just felt a little strange for a moment there."

Lofwyr glanced over his shoulder at Glasgian. "Ah, he does look quite like his father, doesn't he? No wonder it gave you a start. There's no love lost between you and Aithne. Is there?

"I've always wondered about that. It seemed so strange . . ."

"Perhaps some other time," said Caimbeul as he led me away from the dragon.

He steered me about the perimeter of the party,

keeping up a steady flow of nods and polite remarks as we strolled.

"Surehand is just ahead," he said. "Do you think you're up to meeting with him?"

I nodded. "Of course," I said. "It was just a momentary lapse."

Tilting my glass then, I drank the rest of the champagne with one large gulp. A waiter passed close by and I grabbed another glass from him. How I wished it were something stronger.

"You don't suppose Surehand has a supply of Taengele lying about, do you?" I asked.

Caimbeul gave a little frown. I returned it and he knew better than to go over that old ground with me. Oh, I knew that particular demon was never far away, but I didn't succumb to it anymore.

"I'm certain there is little that Lugh denies himself," Caimbeul said. "But we haven't time to indulge that particular vice of yours right now."

I downed the second glass and got a small headache from the bubbles.

"Very well," I said, giving him a grand wave of my hand. "Lead on, MacDuff."

He rolled his eyes, but said nothing as he took my hand and led me to the small circle where Lugh Surehand stood.

"May I present Aina Sluage, Lugh," said Caimbeul.

I extended my hand and Lugh Surehand brought it up to his lips and kissed it. He was much taller than I, with a slender build. His hair was dark red, almost the color of newly turned maple leaves in fall. His eyes were green as summer grass.

I thought he might have looked quite at home in Elizabethan times with his goatee and the rakish scar he sported on his neck. I knew from Caimbeul that it was an old injury, one that ran across and down his neck and across his shoulder.

There was an aura of command about him, though I thought he might have toned it down somewhat to accommodate the temperaments of the other Elders. I suspected that Aithne, Ehran, and the others would never tolerate the idea that they were being led by anyone.

"Ah, so you are Aina," he said. "I have heard so many things about you. How is that we have not met over the years?"

I smiled very slowly at him. "My misfortune, no doubt," I said. "I have always been cursed with bad luck."

"No, madam, the ill fortune was mine," he murmured. He had not yet released my hand.

So that was how it was to be. All so very polite and civilized, until, of course, the knives came out.

"Would you like a tour of the grounds?" Surehand asked.

"Delighted," I said. "I understand they are most impressive."

I let him pull me to his side and tucked my hand into the crook of his elbow. "I am curious," he said as he led me away from the small circle of people and down toward his great house. "I understand you knew Goya. I have always been a great admirer of his work. Tell me, was he mad there at the end?"

I glanced over my shoulder at Caimbeul, but he was already engaged in conversation with a pretty young woman to whom we'd just been introduced, the Countess Teargan. She was Surehand's constant companion, and even Caimbeul was unable to ascertain the nature of their relationship.

"I suppose all humans go mad upon realizing that they will die soon," I said. "Isn't that their great misfortune?"

Surehand glanced at me, his face shrewd for a moment before the pleasant mask slipped back into place.

"I don't believe you find it to be," he said. "I've always found that peculiar about you. You seem to despise your immortal state."

"Despise is a bit strong," I said lightly. "I find the proposition a bit strange. It occurs to me that we few have had so much time, yet we have not done any great good with it. And often we have done such harm in the name of ourselves."

"Perhaps we are beyond such notions as good or bad," he said. We were crossing the broad expanse of green lawn. Lawn that should have been brown this time of year.

"But isn't that the very problem?" I asked.

"So you concern yourself with loftier matters than ours—is that it?" he asked.

I could hear the edge in his voice. "No," I said. "I only know that my choices are those I can live with day to day."

We reached the foot of the wide steps leading up to a terrace outside the house. In the dim light, it looked gray-white and unreal. As though it were some creation conjured up to amaze.

"Yet you come here to ask for my help," he said as he led me up the steps. It was getting colder, and I shivered. He pulled off his jacket and draped it over my shoulders. It smelled of orris root, tobacco, and musk.

"Yes," I said. "I have news that I believe must be told not only to the Elders, but to the world at large."

Pushing open the wide glass doors, Surehand gestured for me to enter the house. Inside it was dark and shadowy. I banged my knee on something and gave a little yelp. Instantly, the room was bathed in golden light.

"It's that damn ottoman," he said. "I keep telling the maids not to leave it here, but they never listen. Are you all right?"

I flopped down on the ottoman and pulled my skirt up to look at the damage. It was minor, but I could tell there would be a bruise the next day.

"It's nothing," I said as I smoothed my skirt back down. "Is it safe to talk here?"

"Yes," he replied. "The house and grounds are swept on a regular basis for any sort of bugging—magical or otherwise. I'm curious, though. You are here with Harlequin. Surely you know he is at odds with Ehran."

"I know," I said. "But his relationship with you is still intact. And I have much more severe problems among the Elders of this Tir myself. Aithne and Alachia, for example. From whom I suspect you have received much of your information about me."

He dropped into a chair opposite me and looked me over.

"You are both not at all what they described and quite like their descriptions," he said after a moment. "But I'm not so foolish as to acquire all my information from only two sources—and those with grudges, no less."

"And what have you found?" I asked. My ego speaking, no doubt.

Surehand settled into his chair, then propped his feet next to me on the ottoman.

"You have stayed out of political dealings for most of this cycle. You disapprove of the way we've been handling matters thus far. According to Aithne, who rarely allows any mention of your name, you are worse than any nightmare."

That stung, coming from someone else. So he hated me enough still to try and sabotage me at every turn. Well, perhaps it was no more than I deserved.

"Ah," I said. "Aithne always did have a way with words."

Lugh Surehand laughed. It was deep and rusty, as though he didn't use it often.

"Alachia underestimates you," he said. "She said you had little wit."

I shrugged. "Alachia underestimates anyone who doesn't automatically worship her—or those who cannot be led around by portions of their anatomy."

"I know little of the animosity between the three of you. Aithne refuses to speak of it, and Alachia holds it out like a trinket, then snatches it away when one gets too close."

I smoothed the velvet of my gown across my knees. In the warm light it took on a deep silver cast. Anything to distract me from memories of the past.

"Do you know the story of Scheherazade?" I asked.

For a moment, Surehand looked startled, but I knew he would quickly replace that with his usual bland expression. I wasn't disappointed. And it occurred to me that for all his show of calmness and balance, he was really quite formidable. After all, he had managed to remain High Prince since the founding of Tir Tairngire. With all the political intrigue so rife among the Elders, he should have been ousted long ago. But here he was in complete control of the Tir.

"She was married to a sultan. He killed every other wife he took after only one night with her," began Surehand. "On the first night of Scheherazade's marriage to him, she refused to lay with him, insisting instead that she would tell him a story. Each night continued after the first the same way. She kept him spellbound with her wit and stories. It continued thus for a thousand nights.

"At the end of the thousand nights, the sultan had fallen in love with Scheherazade and couldn't bring himself to kill her. Thus was she spared."

I clapped my hands softly together. "Bravo," I

said. "Nicely told. You will go far should you ever become the wife of a sultan."

"Am I to take it that you have no desire to become my Scheherazade?"

"I think now would not be the time for those stories. I would not cloud the danger of the present with tales from the past."

"And if I were to insist?"

I shut my eyes. "Then I would oblige," I said.

"Then this must be a very serious matter indeed," he said.

I opened my eyes. He was looking at me with an unreadable expression. I knew then that I would never willingly make an enemy of him. To do so would be far too dangerous, even for me.

"I would not come here otherwise," I said.

"Very well," he said. "What is it you wish?"

"For you to call an emergency meeting of the High Council."

She's in a dark house. At first, she thinks it is Lugh Surehand's mansion, but then she realizes this is no place she's been before.

Outside, she hears the roar of helicopters. Brilliant lights come streaming around the edges of the drawn shades. Then the door bursts open and shadow figures are coming inside. They hold weapons and they are grabbing. Grabbing the other people who are here. There are screams and she starts to run. Run away from the faceless things breaking into her dream.

22

"It went well then?" asked Caimbeul.

We were in the back of the limo again. I still had Surehand's jacket around my shoulders. I'd forgotten to take it off as he led me back to the party.

"He agreed to call a meeting of the High Council," I replied. "It went much better than I expected. But I suspect he'll want something in return."

"And what might that be?"

"I have no idea," I said. "But I think he might be more dangerous than both Aithne and Alachia."

"Lugh Surehand?" Caimbeul was incredulous.

"He's good enough at compromise and juggling the players, but a threat? Please."

Ignoring his arrogance, I stared out the tinted windows. The rain-slick streets flashed by. On a corner I saw a pair of trolls dressed in the height of fashion. I wondered briefly what they were doing here in this neighborhood, then let them fade from my mind.

"You're a fool if you underestimate him, Caimbeul. He has neither Aithne's temper nor Alachia's ego. How has he managed to stay in power all this time? That isn't the feat of someone who should be taken lightly.

"Didn't I read something about an assassination attempt, not too long ago? Despite that, he's still in power. More the wonder if one of us was behind it."

"You sound impressed," he said. "I can't remember the last time anyone impressed you."

"What are you talking about?"

"You sound like a school girl."

"Don't be asinine," I said. I was getting impatient. "You haven't been listening. Yes, I find him interesting, but not in the way you seem to think. He's a force to be reckoned with and not just some puppet put in place by Aithne, Ehran, and Laverty."

Caimbeul made a smug little noise. I turned toward him.

"What was that?" I asked.

"Nothing," he said.

"Why are you making such an issue out of this?"

"You're the one who won't let it drop."

I gave an exasperated sigh and turned away from

him. Sometimes there was no knowing what was in Caimbeul's head.

The main room of the penthouse was dark when we entered. Some pale light filtered in through the terrace windows. The light from the hallway made a wide triangular shape on the floor and cast our shadows long in it.

I banged my injured knee on something and let out a curse. Enough of this, I thought, and caused a light to appear. The room leapt into view, and it took my eyes a moment to adjust to the light.

There, sitting on the couch, was Aithne's son, Glasgian Oakforest.

"Ah, perhaps the very last person I might have expected," said Caimbeul. His voice was pleasant, but I knew from his far too casual stance that he was very angry.

Glasgian stretched and made himself more comfortable. A trick he'd learned from his father.

"My business doesn't concern you, Harlequin," he said. He had a spoiled rich-kid way of speaking. I didn't know who I was more disappointed in—him or Aithne.

"I beg to differ," said Harlequin. "It most certainly is my business when I find an intruder in my hotel room. Besides, aren't you worried about what Daddy would say?"

Glasgian blanched and clenched his fists. That was his father's temper showing. "I've reached my majority, Harlequin. I don't answer to my fa . . . Aithne anymore."

"Stop it, Caimbeul," I said. "Just let him state his business, then he'll be on his way."

"I don't want to talk with him around," said Glasgian.

"Why should I talk to you alone?" I asked.

"Because of who my father is."

"All the more reason not to trust you."

Glasgian began to look a little desperate. What a baby he was, trying so hard to play in a game he didn't even begin to understand.

"Very well," I said. "Caimbeul, I'll deal with him."

"But . . ."

"What can he do?" I asked in Theran. *"He's a child."*

"What better way to get your guard down?"

"Aithne would not sacrifice his son. Not to me."

Caimbeul shrugged, then gave Glasgian one last hard look before casually moving off toward his bedroom.

I slipped off my high-heeled shoes, giving a little sigh as I did so. Murderous things, high heels. Impractical too. Who could run or defend herself in them? I stayed away from them as much as possible.

Ignoring Glasgian for the moment, I went to the portable bar. My feet sank into the thick carpeting and I wriggled my toes against it as I poured myself a healthy snifter of cognac. I didn't bother to ask Glasgian if he wanted any. He'd already helped himself.

I was tired and didn't relish any more verbal wrangling. Lugh Surehand had worn out what little sociability I had in me. What I wanted right now was to be alone. The Council meeting would be held day after tomorrow, and I would need all my energy for that.

I turned and looked Glasgian over. Here, one on one, he seemed less cocksure and full of himself. For a moment, I felt a surge of protectiveness, but I pushed it aside. Those sorts of things were always messy, in my experience.

"What do you want?" I asked. It came out sharper than I'd intended. He looked a bit wounded.

"I . . . I was wondering . . . That is . . . uh . . . What are you to my father?" he blurted out.

I walked over to one of the large armchairs that flanked the couch and sat down. The polished cotton fabric was cool against my back.

"Why do you ask?"

"Because he hates you more than he loves my mother."

"They are separated now, are they not?"

He nodded and looked more like a child than the man he had just become.

"I am his past," I said. "And he would rather not remember it. I don't think anyone reaches a reasonable age without some regrets. Not if you're doing it right."

"But, were you in love? He won't say anything about it. Just that you are something awful. When I saw you, I couldn't believe you were the one he'd been talking about."

"What did you expect? Horns sprouting from my forehead and long fangs?"

"I guess I thought I'd see something that would explain, but all I see is you. And you don't look so terrifying."

I laughed. "I'm surprised you're allowed out on your own, Glasgian. You are refreshingly naive, but I fear you're a bit stupid as well."

He flushed deep red at that.

"Where did you get the rather peculiar idea that you could tell how dangerous someone is by their appearance? Good heavens, not from your father, I'm sure."

"I didn't come here to be insulted," he said.

"No, you came here to invade my privacy and your father's. Not terribly polite of you, if we're counting coup. If that is the reason you came, you'd better go now. I'm tired and I have no patience for indulging a child's curiosity."

I thought this would send him on his way in an indignant huff, but he surprised me. He got up and came toward me, sinking to his knees in front of me. Taking my free hand in his, he brought it to his lips and kissed it. Quite a workout that hand was getting tonight, I thought.

"Do you think you'll send me on my way with insults?" he asked.

"Yes, that was the idea."

"It won't work. I saw how you looked at me when you first saw me. Don't deny it, you wanted me."

I snatched my hand away from him. "Stop it," I said angrily. "This has really gone far enough. I was startled for a moment because you look like your father. For obvious reasons, I didn't want to encounter him."

"Yes, I do look like him," he said softly, leaning toward me until I could smell the whiskey and cinnamon on his breath. "You could pretend I am him. Imagine it, a way to go back and undo the past."

I stood up and stared down at him. How very like Aithne he looked at that moment. But he was only a simulacrum, a faint copy of his father. And twisted in such ways that I wondered at what had caused it.

"What sort of rotten plan do you have in mind?" I asked. "You thought you'd come here, seduce me, then run back to Aithne and throw it in his face. I can't imagine what your father may have done to make you angry enough at him to do such a thing."

Glasgian wrapped his arms around my legs and buried his face in the material of my skirt. "It's more than that," he said. "When I saw you tonight, something happened to me . . . I've never felt like this."

With a quick jerk, I put my knee to his chest. He toppled over, letting go of my dress. I danced away from him, putting several pieces of furniture between us.

"It is only my respect for your father that keeps me from treating you as you deserve. This display was shameful and not worthy of either me or your father. Get out before I lose my temper."

He gave me a smug smile as he straightened his clothes. "It doesn't matter that nothing happened here tonight. I'll tell Aithne it did."

"You are an evil little shit," I said flatly.

He gave me a low bow, but before he could straighten, something caught my attention. Spinning about, I saw that the doors to the terrace had blown open. There, standing in the doorway was the Horror, Ysrthgrathe.

He was as I remembered. Cloaked in deep brown, power radiating off him like a corona. Though his face was shadowed by his hood, I knew how it would appear: cadaverous, with the sienna flesh pulled taut against his skull. The collapsed nose, the yellowed teeth, the heavily muscled arms that burned my flesh as he held it. Under the cloak was his tail. Thick as a man's waist, with protruding bony ridges.

"Ah, I see I must again rescue you from those who would deprive me of my pleasure," Ysrthgrathe said. "You look quite faint, my dear. Is it such a shock to see me again after all this time? I'm wounded. I thought you would have expected me by now."

The air was gone. It felt as though everything was going black. I thought I heard Glasgian's panicked cry, but it seemed to come from some far-off place. I struggled to overcome my panic. In the seconds it took me to regroup, Ysrthgrathe had slid across the floor and grabbed Glasgian.

Backing away from me, he held Glasgian against his chest as a shield. Around Glasgian's neck were Ysrthgrathe's long fingers tipped by razor-sharp nails. Glasgian was making little hiccuping noises.

"Let him go," I said. "This doesn't concern him."

Ysrthgrathe threw back his head and laughed. It bounced off the walls and echoed inside me like a low-throbbing ache.

"Aina, it has indeed been too long. I've missed these little tête-à-têtes. Do you think I don't know who this child is? Come now, I'm not that much of a fool. The irony is almost too perfect. Is it not?" Then he gave a sigh of such perfect rapture that I felt as though a shaft of ice had been driven into my heart.

"How long have you denied me this most perfect of pleasures?" he asked. "I've been waiting for you patiently. You've denied me for far too long. And now you shall pay."

He began to draw his nails across Glasgian's neck. The blood welled up after a moment and trickled down into the white shirt. Glasgian gave a moan, and a dark spot appeared on the front of his trousers and grew.

"Stop it," I shrieked.

Just then, there was a violent flash, a purple jolt of energy, behind Ysrthgrathe. The force of it lifted him and Glasgian off the floor and hurtled them toward me. I dropped to the floor, but still, my shoulder was caught by one of them as they flew by. The force of the impact rolled me over and over until I came to rest against a table.

I looked up and saw Caimbeul standing just beyond the door to his bedroom. There was a crackling of energy around him. Then I heard another sound and turned my head to see what it was. Ysrthgrathe's robes burst into flame. With the briefest nod of the head, he extinguished the flames, and turned to Harlequin with a smile. But he'd also let go of Glasgian, who was making whimpering noises and clutching his throat.

Cursing my long skirts, I struggled to my feet and raced over to him. I pulled his hands away from his neck and looked at the wound. It was bleeding profusely, but wasn't as deep as I'd feared. Placing my hands on the wound, I began to pull the weave of his life together. My hands grew warm, then hot as the magic worked its way into his flesh. Glasgian tried to move away from me, but I tightened my hands and that stopped him.

I heard a cry, and looked up to see Caimbeul falling backwards, arms and legs splayed out. A bright orange flash blinded me for a moment, and when I could see again, Ysrthgrathe stood over Caimbeul. The sweet smell of burning flesh came to me and I fought against the memories it called forth.

I opened my arms, and a blue light leapt between my palms. It coalesced into a ball of blue-white brilliance. Turning my palms outward toward Ysrthgrathe, I pushed the ball away from me. It hurtled across the room and slammed into Ysrthgrathe's side.

The impact spun him around, and then he crashed into the wall with a howl of indignation.

"Ah, Aina," he said, holding his side. "You still care. But despite my gratitude to find that you are as I remember, our sweet reunion must be cut short. I cannot say I approve of your choice of company, but rest assured, I will rectify that in the future."

With that, he vanished.

I sank to the floor just as someone began banging on the door to the penthouse.

No more dreams now.

The nightmares have merged with the waking world. The time for running is over.

Now her sleep is covered by nothing. Nothing except darkness.

23

The pounding at the door continued. Through the thick steel door I could hear a voice calling.

"This is hotel security. Is everything all right in there? If we don't hear an answer in twenty seconds, we're coming in."

"Damn, damn, damn," I muttered as I pushed myself off the floor and stumbled to the door. The left sleeve on my dress was torn, and it slid off my arm. I shoved it up, but it fell down again. Reaching the door, I flung it open.

"What do you want?" I said, trying to keep a balance between annoyance and huskiness in my tone.

"There was a report from the floor below," said one of the uniformed guards. There were two of them—big troll bruisers lugging heavy-duty artillery. "Something about a lot of shooting and banging around. Is everything all right?"

"Of course," I said.

"Mind if we come in?"

"I don't, but my companion might," I said. "He's a bit . . . tied up at the moment." I gave them a hot smoldering look, and one of them looked distinctly uncomfortable.

"Oh . . ."

"But we're always to open to variety," I continued. "I can't remember the last time we had company. That is, if your boss won't mind letting you off-duty for a while."

"Uh . . ."

"Well, what's it to be?"

"I don't think we need to stay. As long as everything is all right."

"We're both fine," I purred. "Really."

The trolls backed away down the hall. I watched them for a moment, then gave them a slow, nasty smile and shut the door.

"What are we going to do about Glasgian?" Caimbeul asked me. He'd just finished off a spell to take care of the wounds he'd suffered in the struggle with Ysrthgrathe.

Unfortunately, Glasgian was in no condition to offer an opinion about his plans. A thin dribble of saliva hung from one corner of his gaping mouth. His eyes were vacant and glassy. When I touched his cheek it was cold and clammy.

"We'll keep him here until after the Council meets. If necessary, we can use him as a demonstration," I said.

"That wouldn't be advisable," replied Caimbeul.

"Aithne," I said.

"Yes."

"Help me with him," I said, taking one of Glasgian's arms.

Together, we managed to drag him to my room and lay him down on the bed. I disconnected the telecom, then cast a spell to protect and hold him. Back in the living room, we righted the furniture toppled during the fight. I went to the terrace doors and shut them.

After a couple of medicinal drinks, I felt more like myself.

"I told you," I said as I finally came to sit beside Caimbeul on the sofa. "I told you he was here. That he'd found a way through." My hands shook and I took another deep drink. And wished for something else. Something more potent.

"I believed you," he said. "But I didn't think the threat was all that great."

"Because you thought you'd already dealt with them. But they're coming like locusts. And they won't stop until they've all made it through."

"Things are different now."

"How?"

"The weapons. The Matrix. And the magic. There is always the magic."

I snorted, then got up to pour myself another drink. "Have you forgotten everything?" I asked. "They learn. They're patient. The first few may die, but there's no end to them."

"Don't you think you've had enough?"

I turned and threw my glass at him. It disappeared a moment before it would have hit his face.

"Aina," he said. "I'm on your side. I just can't stand to see you destroying yourself over this."

"For heaven's sake, Caimbeul, I've just seen the face of my most dreaded enemy after six thousand years, and you're carping about a couple of drinks. It would take far more than that to slow me down right now."

"Pax," he said, holding up his hands. "I want no more fights tonight. One was quite enough. Let's put up a ward, then get some sleep."

"So, are you sleeping on the couch or am I?" I asked.

"Well, it's my bedroom," he said.

"Very well," I replied. "I should have known better than to expect you to be a gentleman about it."

"You're a real pain, you know."

"Oh, I'm fatally wounded," I said. "Do you have an extra blanket?"

He shook his head. "Look, why don't we just share the bed? It's not like we haven't before."

I looked away. "That was different," I said. "It was a long time ago."

"I promise to restrain myself," he said.

"I don't know whether to be flattered or offended."

"You'll be whatever annoys you the most."

I swept by him, going toward his bedroom. "You're right," I said.

* * *

There was more than enough room in the bed for both of us. Three full-sized orks would have been comfortable in it. Despite, or maybe because of, Caimbeul's promise, I couldn't sleep. I'd been afraid to sleep because of the dreams. But now I suspected there would be no more dreams.

Ysrthgrathe, my old enemy. More faithful than any lover. The weight of my past with him hung in my mind. I shut my eyes, but images kept coming to me. The trail of death and blood that followed me because of him.

A sick feeling settled into my stomach and worked its way up my throat. I shuddered at the thought of the pain and suffering that I knew Ysrthgrathe would inflict. All in my name.

A low moan escaped my lips.

"Aina," said Caimbeul.

"Did I wake you?" I asked. "I'm sorry."

"No," he said. "I can't sleep. I'm feeling cold. Do you mind if I hold you? Strictly for warmth."

I slid across the vast expanse of the bed into the warmth of his arms. And still it was many hours before I slept.

A banging woke me the next morning.

"Doesn't anyone just knock in this hotel?" asked Caimbeul. We were tangled up together, just like we used to be in other, happier times. He threw off the covers and grabbed his robe from the edge of the bed.

I pulled the covers up over my head and tried to go back to sleep, but then I remembered where I was and what that meant. With a groan, I threw the covers off and made my way to the bathroom.

Just as I shut the door, I heard the sound of voices, so I poked my head out.

"What? Surprised to see me?"

Ehran.

I groaned. More bad luck. But wasn't that always the case? I rummaged through Caimbeul's suitcase and found a shirt, a pair of pants, and a belt. Not fashionable, but it would have to do.

As I pushed open the door leading to the living room, I could see them squaring off against one another, even though they would never actually do anything here.

"Well, well," I said brightly, stepping into the room. "Ehran, won't you join us for breakfast?"

"Aina," he said. "It's been a long time."

"Isn't it always?" I replied. "I know the two of you are just dying to go at one another, but I'm really famished. I'll call down. What are you in the mood for?"

"Answers," Ehran said.

"I don't think that's on the menu."

He jerked his thumb toward Caimbeul. "Why do you spend so much of your time with him?" I half expected Caimbeul to take the bait, but he only glared back at his old rival. Maybe he was keeping quiet because he knew how important all of this was to me.

"Slumming," I said. "It keeps me off the streets. Really, Ehran, who knows why certain people always seem to end up together?"

"Then tell me why you're both here. And why did you have a meeting with Lugh Surehand last night? Which seems to have resulted in an emergency meeting of the High Council being called."

"Good heavens, Ehran," I said. "With spies that good, why do you need to come to us?"

"When I found out you were here as well as *him,* I decided to come," Ehran said.

I opened the room service menu and glanced over the selections. "Really, Ehran, I'm touched, but we've never been close. And only rarely allied. Why come?"

"Don't try to discuss anything with him, Aina," said Caimbeul. While Ehran and I had been talking, he'd walked to the window and pulled open the drapes. Weak sunlight filled the room. The sky was overcast and looked like it might rain.

"Don't listen to him, Aina," said Ehran. "He just thinks—"

"Would you both shut up?" I nearly shouted. "Haven't you grown tired of all this bickering? There are more important matters at stake than your interminable feud."

"Well, now we're getting down to it," said Ehran.

"For heaven's sake, Aina," said Caimbeul. "Don't breathe a word to him. He'll go running to everyone else quick as you please, and you'll be sunk before you've had a fair hearing."

Then they were off and running. Nothing ever got solved between the two of them—it was still that old business. I confess, my sympathies lay with Caimbeul—he was the aggrieved party, after all—but that's another story, for another time.

I waited until they ran out of steam, which they eventually did. They sat at opposite ends of the room glowering at each other.

"So," I said. "What would you both like for breakfast?"

"Why won't you tell me?" Ehran asked for perhaps the thirtieth time.

I wiped my mouth with the napkin and dropped it onto my empty plate with the remains of the lavish breakfast we'd ordered. Caimbeul had loaded a plate with food, then disappeared into his bedroom. Pouring myself another cup of coffee—the real stuff, not that awful soykaf—I got up and went to one of the large armchairs and plopped down on it.

"First, because you and Aithne are long-time friends. I suspect anything you hear from me goes straight back to him. Second, you're also close to Alachia. Oh, don't give me the surprised look. I know she's been a member of the Council since the beginning. You were smart to try to keep that secret, though. There are still a few of us who remember the old days.

"I would hate to think what might happen should Alachia's influence become more . . . assertive. I believe things might get very difficult indeed. Just remember, Lofwyr is keeping an eye on things."

Ehran didn't say anything, but leaned back in his chair and lit a cigarette. I got up and went to open the terrace doors. Nasty habit, that. I'd taken it up briefly and put it aside as quickly. The Indians had the right idea about tobacco. It wasn't a thing to be taken casually. They understood that. Unfortunately, the Europeans didn't.

"I might think that there was a threat in what you're saying," said Ehran.

"No," I said softly. "I don't threaten. You know better than that. I'm just letting you know my position."

"Don't you think it's a bad idea to alienate me right before the meeting of the Council?" He blew little smoke rings and watched them float away from him.

"I know you're willing to hear the truth. And that you might be willing to overlook my unfortunate choice in companions."

Ehran smiled at me. "I've always liked you, despite your strange politics."

"That and Aithne."

"Yes," he said. "We've all made enemies of one another over the years. It comes from time and contact. Such a terrible thing—to be bound together over such a span. Do you sometimes grow weary?"

"Oh, yes," I said. I rose from my chair and went to the terrace doors to close them. Now that Ehran had finished with his cigarette, I found the chill air more than I could bear. It seeped into my bones today. I tried to blame it on the humidity, the gray sky, the wind.

"Sometimes," he said softly, "I wonder if we all don't go a little mad from it. In our own ways, of course."

"How so?"

"Harlequin's and my ongoing quarrel. Alachia's actions in Blood Wood. Your own rejection of your people for the Great Worms. Are not all of these insanity?"

"It all depends on where you're looking from," I replied.

He pushed himself away from the table. "I won't say anything to anyone about your being here," he said. "You may count on my discretion. By the way, whatever happened to young Oakforest? Glasgian, you remember? He was seen coming up here, then he never came out. Where is he?"

"I have no idea what you're talking about," I said. "Maybe your spies got it wrong."

"I doubt it. They're quite good at this sort of thing."

"Well, he's not here."

"Then you won't mind if I take a look—"

"Yes, I would," I said quickly. "You're treading a fine line here, Ehran. Even if he were here, which he's not, it wouldn't be any of your business. Let's leave it at that. Shall we?"

He gave another faint smile. "Very well, Aina," he said. "But this is a dangerous game you're playing."

I walked to the door and opened it. "I know, but when has it ever not been?"

As soon as the door shut, Caimbeul opened the door to his room and peered out.

"I thought he'd never leave," he said.

"I can't believe you left me here to deal with him," I said. "And he knows about Glasgian."

"Yes, I heard that."

"Well, we've got to get him out of here," I said. "I just don't know if he's up to anything but the conventional means."

"We may have no other choice."

I nodded, then turned and walked over to my bedroom door and opened it. The room was still dark, the shades pulled. A wedge of light from the living room spilled across the bed, which was empty. I hit the switch on the wall, flooding the room with electric light.

The room was empty. Glasgian Oakforest was gone.

24

"He's gone," I said.

"What?"

"He's gone."

Caimbeul elbowed past me into the room.

"Maybe the bathroom?" he asked.

I pointed to the open bathroom door. "Unless he's thinner than I remember. Or he's hiding in the shower stall."

Caimbeul went and checked in the stall. "No, not here."

I sagged against the dresser facing the bed. "This is very bad," I said. "What if he goes to Aithne? We're lost then."

"I don't think he'll do that," Caimbeul said. He touched the bed where Glasgian had lain. "It's cold. He's probably been gone for a while. I suspect he didn't leave by the usual methods, because otherwise Ehran wouldn't have asked about him."

"Maybe Ehran took him," I said.

Caimbeul shook his head. "Not his style. Now, I'd expect it from Alachia, except she'd be here now crowing about it. And I don't think her network is as sophisticated as Ehran's. What surprises me is that we haven't heard from Aithne yet."

"Dumb luck," I said. "What are we going to do?"

"Nothing," he replied. "For right now. Whoever has him will show their hand eventually, and if he got out of here himself, then I doubt we'll hear anything. He'll be too damn scared. After all, he's had a look at what happens to people who get on the wrong side of your faithful companion."

"Don't call him that," I snapped. "I haven't seen him in millennia. I took care of him long ago. You know that. I'm tired of paying for that mistake. It won't just be me facing him this time. I'll have the support of the others."

Caimbeul shrugged. "Perhaps," he said. "There's no telling what they'll do."

I ran a hand across my scalp. "They've got to see what's happening. After you tell them about Maui, they'll understand. But what has me worried is how anyone got past those wards."

Caimbeul didn't say anything.

The rest of the day dragged on interminably. After the way the morning went, I kept expecting more unwelcome visitors. But they never arrived.

The maids came and tidied the rooms, and I wondered which one of them was Ehran's spy. Or maybe all of them were.

I jumped at every noise, and Caimbeul's annoying habits became more and more glaring. Pencil-tapping. Humming. Leg-jiggling. He twitched and fidgeted and moved around like a six-year-old need-ing to pee.

I wondered why I'd ever had anything to do with him.

The day of the Council meeting dawned clear and cold. The drizzle and gray skies that had continued for the last two days broke. It irked me that the ses-sion had been set up for late afternoon. I had to waste yet another day with the tension, boredom, and Caimbeul's habits.

At four we began to get ready, and by five we were in the rented limo heading for the meeting. It was already beginning to grow dark as we finally reached the estate where the meeting was to take place.

It was located west of the city. As the car swung into the wide gates flanking the drive, I saw that there were hundreds of rose bushes lining the drive. They were denuded of foliage. Their thorny canes stark and skeletal against the fading October sky.

Several other limos were parked in front of the large house as we pulled up. There were also a cou-ple of high-octane performance cars modified with body armor.

"Looks like the joint's jumpin'," said Harlequin. "Nice cars. I wonder who they belong to."

"Jinkies, Caimbeul, maybe you and the boys can go drag racing after the sock hop," I said.

"You don't have to get snippy about it," he said.

"You're a gadabout," I said. "Utterly irresponsible. Can't you keep your mind on the matter at hand?"

"Why should I?" he asked. "When you're perfectly capable of doing all the worrying for both of us."

"Jerk."

"Shrew."

"Shmuck."

"Harpy."

I laughed. I couldn't help it.

"Well, shall we go and meet the crowd?" Caimbeul asked. "I understand they've finished with the pagans and are moving on to the Christians."

"I think they'll find us stringy and unpalatable."

"One can only hope."

We were met at the door by a retinue of Surehand's Paladins. They were attired in their Crusader-ish armor and toting SMGs, pistols, and other sidearms and pieces of gear I knew nothing of. Such blind reliance on technology could get these boys in a lot of trouble, I thought.

We were escorted into the massive foyer and down a wide hallway leading to the back of the house. More like a palace. Fifteen-foot ceilings, twelve-foot-wide hallways, heavy, cream-colored damask wallpaper, marble tile underfoot. The Paladins' boots made loud echoes against the floor. Doorways leading off the halls showed enormous rooms decorated in luxurious fabrics, woods, and stone.

I wondered whose property this was. It dwarfed Lugh Surehand's place in size and richness. I couldn't imagine Aithne here. Nor Ehran. It hardly seemed their style. Our invitation to the Council had mentioned only the time and location: six p.m. at Ozymandias. Caimbeul seemed to know where to go.

At last we came to a set of doors at the end of the hallway. The lead Paladin opened the doors and announced us.

"Aina Sluage and Caimbeul har lea Quinn," he said.

I took a deep breath and stepped into the room. Caimbeul was close behind.

Had I been Harlequin, I would have delighted at the expressions passing over those faces, but I was too nervous. I knew they wouldn't guess how I felt. None of them knew me well enough to see that.

"Courage," I heard Caimbeul whisper in my ear.

Fires burned in the hearths at either end of the hall. Oriental rugs were scattered over the inlaid wood floor. Oversized chairs and couches were arranged in comfortable groupings. That is, comfortable if you're expecting a hundred or so of your closest personal friends.

At one end of the hall were a handful of the Council members. Lofwyr had changed from his black suit into a lurid peacock-blue satin that would have done a pimp proud. He smiled and bowed slightly at me. I knew he'd probably remain neutral, no matter what happened. Sometimes you just couldn't depend on dragons.

Ehran was ensconced on one of the couches. He wore his usual black, a habit that I found a trifle annoying. As though wearing black made you somehow more imposing, or cool, or serious. Though it did contrast nicely with his white hair and cold blue eyes. We made eye contact, but I couldn't tell what he was thinking. It was as though our meeting the other day had never taken place.

Sean Laverty was perched on the arm of one of the chairs. Unlike the other men, he was clean-shaven. His eyes were clear leaf-green, his hair auburn. I knew he was against the technological leanings of the Tir. Of the group, his garb was the simplest. A T-shirt and jeans with a jacket thrown on top. In one earlobe he wore a dangling silver dragon. I wondered what Lofwyr made of that.

Sitting in the chair was Jenna Ni-Fairra. She was whispering something to Laverty as I approached the group.

"Sean, Jenna," I said.

"Aina," they replied in unison. I wondered for a moment if they were joined at the hip.

"Did anyone miss me?" came a voice behind me. An all too familiar voice. I turned. Alachia. She glided over to Jenna and kissed her cheek. They were remarkably alike. Except for the coloring, they could have been twins. Where Alachia's hair was deep red, Jenna's was platinum blond. Alachia's eyes were clear sapphire blue; Jenna's emerald green. But the face was the same. Delicate and fey. Unearthly beauty. What a bore.

"Why must you wear these things?" asked Alachia, grabbing Jenna's black leather jacket and giving it a shake. "Upstairs I know you have a closet full of . . ."

Jenna gave her a hard look, and Alachia laughed it off. "A mother's prerogative," she said lightly. She glanced around the room. "Well, it looks as if we're almost all here."

Just then there was the sound of raised voices coming down the hall. We all turned. In a moment, the doors flew open. Aithne burst in with the Paladin guard hot on his heels. They tried to slow him down, but he thrust one hand up behind him and they flew back into the hall.

"What the hell were you thinking of with those damn roses?" said Aithne. "Alachia, if this is your sick idea of a jok—"

Then he saw me.

His face had been flushed. Now it went white.

"What the frag is she doing here?" he asked. His voice was cold. Utterly devoid of emotion.

"Isn't it the nicest surprise?" said Alachia, coming up next to him and tucking her arm in his. "Aina asked Lugh to call a meeting of the Council. And he agreed." She leaned against Aithne and beamed at me.

I wanted to throttle her.

"I'm leaving," he said. "There is nothing *that* woman can say that will interest me in the least."

He swung around and headed toward the door.

"You'd best not go," said Surehand. "I would look unfavorably upon it."

Aithne stopped, then turned again, slowly.

"And what is that supposed to be?" Aithne asked. "A threat?"

"No," replied Surehand. "I don't want you to let old personal matters hinder your judgment of these events. If you leave, you give tacit approval to anything we decide."

"Not if I leave under protest."

"The result will be the same. We will make a decision, and you will have to live with it."

Aithne glared at Surehand for a long moment.

"Very well. This woman," he said, pointing at me, "is a treacherous bitch and nothing she says can be trusted."

"So much for the impartial hearing," murmured Caimbeul.

"Your taste in companions leaves much to be desired," Aithne said to Caimbeul.

"People in glass houses," replied Caimbeul, looking pointedly at Alachia. Aithne glanced down and saw she was still attached to his arm. He jerked his arm away and stalked to one of the large arm chairs, where he flung himself down.

"All right," he said. "What's this all about?"

"Aina," said Lugh. "If you please."

Caimbeul gave me a little pat on the back, then went and took a seat on the couch next to Ehran. They began a subtle war of who could sprawl on the couch most. Aithne refused to look at me, while Jenna and Sean whispered and giggled.

"As you all know," I began, "the magical forces have been on an upsurge for the past fifty or so years. Many of the old ways have returned, though there have been some unforeseen changes due to the technological state of this cycle. But that is neither here nor there.

"In the past, great surges of magic have drawn the Enemy to this place. The Therans solved this by leading the world into the darkness of the kaers for five hundred years. But we all know the prices paid for those choices."

I paused for a moment and glanced around the room. Ehran's expression was carefully blank. Caimbeul gave me a little wink. Alachia yawned and looked bored.

"There have been two serious encounters with the Enemy in past months," I said. "Caimbeul defeated them on the metaplanes. Then, more recently, he told me about the encounter on Maui where the Enemy actually managed to get through a portal opened by kahunas of a tribe there during one of their blood rituals."

"Did he say he actually drove them back?" asked Ehran. "Aina, you know how he likes to take credit for things he had nothing to do with."

"I don't recall you being there," said Caimbeul.

"News travels fast, Harlequin," said Ehran. "You always were a braggart."

"Would you both just stop," I said. I paced a bit.

This was why I avoided them. All this petty bickering. We'd been in and out of each other's lives for so long that everyone knew each other's sore spots. Where to poke and prod. And yet, we still kept coming together again.

"Who did what isn't important," I said. "The point is, the Enemy is coming back. And they're coming too soon. This world isn't ready. Its people don't understand a damn thing about what's happening. And we certainly haven't prepared them."

"What do you think the Tir is?" asked Alachia. "We're creating a place where the strong will survive."

"You mean where the elves will survive and everyone else on the planet can shift for themselves," I said.

"What's wrong with that?" asked Jenna, ever her mother's daughter.

"Well, if you don't mind billions of innocent people suffering unimaginable deaths," I said.

"Innocent blood has never bothered you before," interjected Aithne.

I looked at him and narrowed my eyes. As though his loss had been greater than mine.

"Things change," I said at last. "So do people. Most people. But this is all beside the point. This isn't some academic discussion. I believe that one of the Enemy is already here. I don't know how he managed to come across. Perhaps in Maui. Or maybe there is another point of entry. All I know is that he is here."

There was a hush for a moment, then everyone began to ask questions. Lugh called for them to calm down.

"How do you know it's the Enemy?" Lugh asked.

"He has contacted me," I said. "First, there were dreams. Then I received a telecom communication. Two nights ago he attacked us in our hotel room here in Portland."

"What do you know about this, Harlequin?" asked Surehand.

"Just what Aina has told you. You know about the events in Maui," he said. This surprised me. I didn't know he'd told them about Maui. "I was there when the call came to Aina's place in Scotland. And I was there when it attacked us in the hotel room."

"Perhaps it's just one," said Sean. "It would be easy enough to deal with."

"I don't see what the big fuss is about," said Alachia. "We've defeated them before. We'll defeat them again."

"Haven't you heard a word I've said?" I asked. "It's too early for them to be coming through. We're not ready. The world isn't ready. You've spent so much time playing at politics and nations that you've neglected the important things. It's as though we've left nuclear weapons for cavemen to play with. These people don't understand what's at stake. And they certainly don't comprehend the nature of the powers they're dealing with."

"Now we get down to it," crowed Alachia. "All

228

this time going on about how much more pure and noble you are than us. You just don't want anyone using the power. What's the matter, Aina, scared someone will tread on your magical toes?"

I glanced over at Caimbeul, but he was busy trying to annoy Ehran. "No," I said. "But these magical spikes seem to be attracting the Enemy. As long as people capriciously use blood magic, the risk will grow."

"You would know about blood magic," said Aithne.

"Yes, and you should be smart enough to lay aside your hatred of me to see the larger issue at hand. We must stop this one and prevent the rest from coming through."

"I think you're overestimating the danger," interjected Alachia. "Perhaps *your* experience is tinting your perspective."

"Besides, we have plans," said Laverty. "Now is not a good time to reveal such secrets."

"Have I been shut up with a bunch of lunatics?" I shouted. "You don't pick when the Enemy comes. They *will* come when the circumstances are right. The best we can do is slow that event down. Which means we must act now."

I stopped then, realizing they weren't listening to me. They were staring gape-mouthed at something behind me. Slowly, I turned.

A vortex of smoke was whirling up out of the floor in front of the fireplace. A shape uncoiled from inside the smoke and stepped forward. Ysrthgrathe. Hanging limply in his arms was Glasgian Oakforest.

"I do so love to make an entrance," he said as he dropped Glasgian on the floor. "But I know better than to overstay my welcome. Aina, it is so good to see you again. See, I've brought you a little present. I shall see you soon, my dear. 'Til we meet again."

Then he disappeared.

Lances of arcane fire cut through the space where he'd been a moment before. Aithne rushed to Glasgian's side. Surehand called for his Paladins. Sean and Jenna hovered behind Aithne asking if they could help. Ehran and Caimbeul had that odd, distracted look in their eyes, the faintest traces of energy crackling around them.

I turned away from the sight of Aithne holding Glasgian's limp body. It was then that I saw Alachia's face. She had a small, knowing smirk on her face. And a notion so terrible filled my mind that I immediately pushed it away. I couldn't think such a thing. Not even of her.

I spun away from the sight of her. Now Glasgian seemed to be coming around. When he saw that he was in his father's arms, his face crumpled and he began to cry. Aithne cooed and cradled Glasgian in his arms until his sobs diminished into irregular hiccups. At last, Glasgian seemed to fall into another kind of stupor.

Surehand suggested that Aithne have Glasgian carried up to a room, but Aithne refused and hugged Glasgian tightly to him.

"This is all your doing," he hissed at me. "This sort of thing follows wherever you go. I knew we shouldn't ever have anything to do with you again."

"For heaven's sake, Aithne," said Lofwyr. "She didn't bring it here."

"Yes, she did," he said. "That creature has followed her through space and time. It will destroy anyone around her. This isn't *the* Enemy. It's *her* enemy. It has come for her and I say we let it have her. She seeks to divert the issue. But we must see it for what it is. This is Aina's battle. Not ours. Let her deal with it."

"I must agree with Aithne," said Alachia. "Obviously, Aina wants us to become involved with this personal matter. We don't know that she didn't conjure it up herself. After all, that was a specialty of hers, as I recall. This isn't about the world—it's about her.

"She has turned her back on us. I say we let her shift for herself."

I had my back to her, but I knew she had plastered a noble, righteously dignified expression on her face.

Now they all would agree with her.

"This is a terrible mistake," I said. "If I cannot stop him, he will bring them all across. He has the power to do so."

"Get her out of here," snarled Aithne. "If she says one more word I think I'll . . ."

Caimbeul came and wrapped his jacket around me. I hadn't realized I'd been shivering.

"Let's go," he said.

"But . . ."

"You've done all you could," he said.

I let him lead me from the room. Our footsteps echoed down the long hallway as we left.

25

"What am I going to do?" I asked.

I was huddled in the back of the limo. Caimbeul gave the driver instructions to take us straight to the airport.

"We'd best get out of here as quickly as possible," he said.

"What about our things at the hotel?" I asked.

"Leave them," he replied. "It's just clothes."

"Where are we going?"

"I don't know. The next possible flight out. I don't want Aithne or Alachia thinking they might want to have us arrested."

"Arrested? What could they possibly arrest us for?"

"You name it. All they have to do is convince Lugh to send out the order. They could lock us up and keep us locked up for a long time. Have you forgotten when Alachia kept you imprisoned before? They would be able to justify it."

I shoved my hands into the pockets of my jacket. I'd failed, I thought. They'd rejected me and my warnings. Now I would have to face Ysrthgrathe by myself. I didn't know if I had the strength to fight him again.

The limo's headlights illuminated row after row of dormant rose bushes.

Thorns.

So many thorns.

The first flight we could book passage on was a small tour plane. They were doing a hop from Portland to Eugene, then on to a small airstrip near Crater Lake. After refueling there, the next leg was to Eureka.

I hated small planes even more than large ones. So many things to go wrong, none of which I had any control over. How loathsome.

Luckily, the leg from Portland to Eugene was quiet. While Caimbeul and I stretched our legs, they took on more passengers. Lots of back-to-nature types. A couple of humans who said they were going to Crater Lake to perform research. The rest were elves. Judging from their totems and tattoos, they all appeared to be involved with some kind of shamanistic magic.

This annoyed me. These shamans.

"Do you see?" I asked Caimbeul in a low whisper. "They just don't see the large way of things. With them it's all power conferred through something else. They don't see that the power is in them."

"You can't make them other than what they are," Caimbeul said. "They were shaped by a world where magic didn't exist. Their understanding of it will always be limited. Maybe the next generation . . ."

I frowned. "If we don't stop Ysrthgrathe, there might not be another generation."

The plane circled over Crater Lake before landing on the small airstrip about five miles away. The shamans and the humans all filed off with their backpacks. I knew that Crater Lake had been sealed off for some time by the military. It amazed me that anyone would try to get close to it without some sort of clearance.

Then it occurred to me—how stupid I was—that they just might have clearance. If what Dunkelzahn had told me about Crater Lake was true, then the Tir could very well be pulling in magicians here and there to help them.

Caimbeul and I also got out at this stop. There was a two-hour layover. We followed the others into the tiny terminal. It was just one large room with a few benches. Through the plate glass window I saw two army jeeps with soldiers waiting outside. The shamans and the humans went immediately to them, gave some papers to the soldiers, then piled into the jeeps.

"How much do you know about what's happening down there at Crater Lake?" I asked Caimbeul.

"Enough to know it would only upset you," he replied. "Are you hungry?"

I nodded. "Starved," I said. "But it looks like there are only those vending machines over there.

Stale, dried miso soup, dehydrated beans and rice, maybe an old candy bar."

"Have no fear, madam," he said. "We have two hours, and I happen to know of a place nearby that has fabulous food and a hell of a view."

He led me outside and hailed what had to be the only taxi for five counties. The driver actually agreed to let us hire him for the next two hours. Caimbeul gave him the name of the restaurant, and we were off.

He hadn't lied about the view. We were at the top of one of the higher peaks in the area. From this vantage we could see the surrounding countryside. Off in the distance was a blue glow that made me very nervous.

"Is that what I think it is?" I asked Caimbeul.

"Shhh, no questions now," he said. "Just have something to eat and think about getting out of here after dinner. We'll talk later."

It annoyed me, but perhaps he was right. No matter what was happening, I couldn't stop it. Not now, at any rate.

Slowly, I began to relax. There were mostly military types in the restaurant. Some civilians, but they looked to be locals. It was an old-fashioned Mom and Pop kind of place. Mostly vegan dishes, with one or two meat entrees for the non-elven types. Given the makeup of the crowd, I suspected they didn't do a lot of business with the beef.

No one gave us much of a second glance. A little odd, unless they were used to seeing strangers.

Caimbeul ordered some wine, but I declined. I wanted to be as sharp as possible until we made it out of the Tir. We lingered a bit over dessert, but then it was time to head back to the airstrip.

Our driver had apparently gotten something from the kitchen, because the cab smelled of eggplant ratatouille.

I shut my eyes as the cab headed away from the restaurant and down the hill. I must have dozed off for a moment, because the next thing I remember was being thrown to the floor. Caimbeul was cursing; the driver was screaming.

"What's happening?" I yelled as I pushed myself off the floor.

"Keep going!" shouted Caimbeul.

The driver didn't answer but continued to scream. I poked my head up, trying to see what was going on. The driver reached forward and pulled something from under the seat. A gun. Still yelling, he began to fire it through the window. Just as he shot, I looked.

There, illuminated by the cab's headlights, was Ysrthgrathe standing in the middle of the road. Then the glass shattered, and he was broken into a million fragmented images.

I grabbed the door handle and yanked. It flew open and I fell out after it, sprawling on the rough asphalt of the road on my hands and knees.

"Ah, Aina," Ysrthgrathe said. "Don't you remember? You don't have to kneel to me."

I pushed myself off the ground. There were scrapes on my hands. The blood welled out of them and stung. In the distance I could hear something. I thought it sounded like a baby's cry. Then I realized it was the driver.

"Most annoying, that noise," said Ysrthgrathe. In a flash, he slid across the small distance between him and the driver's door. Ripping the door off its hinges, he then pulled the driver out by his neck. Slowly, he began to squeeze.

The driver's face turned red, then purple. His eyes began to bulge, and he grabbed frantically at his neck. His feet began to spasm and became entangled in Ysrthgrathe's robe.

"This is certainly sweet," said Ysrthgrathe. "But it really isn't up to my usual. Of course, I have only the faintest memories of that, now. You have deprived me for so long. And you're not nearly as fond of this one as you might be. Perhaps the other . . ."

He closed his hand then, and I heard the bones in the driver's neck snap and pop like firecrackers. Then Ysrthgrathe tossed him away like a used-up toy.

Caimbeul emerged from the back of the passenger side of the cab then. He had a black eye and a nasty cut on his lip. It was beginning to swell, making his mouth look lopsided. It looked like he hadn't fully recovered his senses.

"Go," I said. "He wants me."

Caimbeul shook his head. "He can't possibly deal with both of us. Not now."

"You should listen to her," said Ysrthgrathe. "But then, I wouldn't have as much fun if you leave. I can taste how she cares for you. Her fear for your safety is so sweet, but really, I must have more."

With that, he pushed his arms forward. A solid beam of black energy shot out from them. It hit Caimbeul full in the chest, sending him flying backwards. I heard him cry out in pain and could smell the odor of burning clothes and skin.

"No!" I shouted.

His eyes glowed and he smiled. Another lash of energy cracked like whip and I heard the bones of Caimbeul's legs snap.

"No!" I screamed again. Was he going to break Caimbeul bone by bone?

Then there was a roaring in my ears, like the sound of jet engines. The blood was warm in my hands. It tickled me. Calling to me. Asking me to come and play again. To use it as I once had.

I dug my nails into my palms, wincing slightly, and then I spoke the words. A language long dead to this modern world. My mother tongue, that had never left me and that would always be my secret heart.

Ribbons of blood danced from my fingertips and wove themselves around Ysrthgrathe. He roared in anger at this, but I laughed. Oh, I had been careful for so long. It felt wonderful to let the power out. To revel in it again. I let it take hold of me. Slide through me. Fill me. Fill the void inside.

Soon, Ysrthgrathe was encased in a blood-cocoon. Using one hand to control the cocoon, with the other I began to cast another spell. But Ysrthgrathe wasn't so easily controlled. He shot into the air, dragging me along. We flew above the trees, and the upper branches scratched and scraped at my legs.

I grabbed at the blood ribbons with both hands to steady myself. *What is he up to?* I wondered. I looked about and saw that he was flying us straight toward Crater Lake.

If we went much further, we'd be shot down by the Tir military for certain. Cursing, I let go of the blood ribbons. Ysrthgrathe shot ahead, and I fell. I was battered and bruised by tree limbs. It took me a moment before I could cast a flying spell.

I flew up to the top of the trees and peered around.

"Looking for me?" came Ysrthgrathe's voice above me.

I looked up. His head was free from the cocoon, but the rest of his body was still encased. He spat out some words, and the cocoon shattered. It sent drops of blood flying everywhere. My face and clothes were spattered with it.

"What's that old saying?" Ysrthgrathe asked. "Fool me once, shame on you. Fool me twice, shame on me?"

I didn't reply, just furiously tore at my wrist with my teeth. How I yearned for a knife at that moment. Oh, for the power I'd lost. For the power to come.

"This is most annoying," Ysrthgrathe said. "You've changed. You're not at all like you were before.

"Where is your fear? It was so sweet and delicious. Your pain? Your agony? Have you forgotten the dark years of your torment already? I remember them as if they were yesterday.

"Your pain, my pleasure. Think of what I can offer you. Don't you recall? The power. Imagine what you could be here with that power now. They would be forced to listen to you. You could make them bend to your will. They would have to do your bidding."

And I was tempted.

It had been so many years since I'd felt anything close to the sensation of the power. Such a unity of self and soul. Body and mind. Maybe only the absinthe had come close. But even that joy was fleeting.

My blood sang to be used. To be taken again. From Crater Lake I could feel the pull of even greater power. It sang to me.

Take me.

Use me.

"Yes," he said. "Think of it. This world can't even imagine what the power is. They play at magic like a game. They don't understand. But you do, Aina. You've always understood the true nature of the gift. It's in your blood. Take my gift."

A foolish mistake.

I hadn't thought him so clumsy. So obvious. To go over old ground again.

"Oh, dear," I said. "What was it you said? Fool me once . . ."

The blood had been running into my palms. It writhed, then began to whirl. It bubbled over my fingertips and began to slide toward the ground. It wanted me to use it.

It craved that.

I craved that.

So I let us have what we wanted.

From over the horizon, the blue glow from Crater Lake became brighter. The power surged into me. And this time, this time, I didn't refuse it.

The spell burst out of me. It sang and jumped from my lips. Insects flew into the sky in a great cloud. The bones of long-dead animals rose up and began to circle about Ysrthgrathe. The insects joined them, and soon the blood danced out of my hands and mingled with the bones and insects.

Surrounding Ysrthgrathe. Encasing him.

"Aina," he said. His voice was a soft whisper, but somehow I could hear it above the buzzing of the wasps. It was inside me. In my mind, like someone lurking at a window. "Aina, don't turn me away. I shan't forgive you this time. This time I will take everything away."

"Go ahead and try," I said. I released the spell then. Let it surge out of me. Out of my soul. Out of the centuries of solitude and loneliness. From the pain of my loss and sadness.

And, oh, it made such a lovely sight.

Ysrthgrathe became darker and darker, until I felt as if the very light was being drawn into him. Then, in the matter of a nanosecond, there was an immense radiance that blinded me.

When I could see again, there was nothing left of the insects, or the bones, or the blood, or of

Ysrthgrathe. In the sky there was the faint azure glow from Crater Lake, dimmer this time.

Then, there was only the faint twinkling of the stars.

26

"Where will you go now?" asked Caimbeul.

We were standing in the Orly airport. It was some three weeks after I'd faced Ysrthgrathe for the last time.

I had found Caimbeul unconscious from the blow Ysrthgrathe had given him. I'd healed him, and then we'd gone looking for the authorities to notify them about the cab driver's death. The tale Caimbeul had spun was impressive, even by his usual standards.

We finally got out of Tir Tairngire the next day.

I contacted Dunkelzahn and told him about what had happened. In dragon-like fashion, he merely nodded and accepted what I said. If he had any other opinions, he kept them to himself. Though he did invite me to stay and visit.

Caimbeul and I decided to go to the Riviera. Perhaps it was the foolishness of age, but we both thought there might still be something between us.

By the time we parted at Orly, we knew that whatever had been there was best left in the past.

"Where will you go now?" he asked again.

"I think I shall travel for a bit," I said. "No place

too interesting. I think I've had enough interesting things in my life for a while. I know that one day the Enemy will come again, but now that Ysrthgrathe is gone, I feel . . . safer.

"Maybe they were right. Maybe it was my problem. Perhaps I've been wrong."

Caimbeul shrugged. He'd become very Gaelic during our visit.

"I've always thought your instincts were pretty good," he said. He reached out and pulled me to him. The kiss he gave me was long, and hot, and bittersweet.

It was some six months later that I made it back to Arran.

It was spring.

The land had turned green again. The wind blew from the south, bringing the delicate odor of grass, peat, and heather to me.

I opened the house up, flinging wide the windows to drive out the inevitable mustiness. Caimbeul had stayed here at some point while I was gone. I saw a few things were out of place. How like him, I thought.

I tapped the print bar on my telecom, and material began to spew out.

Since I'd put a hold on the dailies and the magazines, I wondered what this glut could be.

Frowning, I picked up the first sheet. It was an article about Aztechnology. There were numerous articles about Aztechnology. They came from mainline papers as well as obscure, paranoid, end-of-the-world publications. Shaking my head, I read another and another and another.

There were articles about many unrelated events. They were scattered across the globe, and these articles were in Chinese, French, German, Swahili, Japanese, and many other languages.

Mostly, they were about random occurrences of mania. A woman goes crazy and kills her children. There is no explanation and she doesn't remember the event even happening. Later, she takes her own life, scrawling images of obscene monsters in her own blood on the prison walls.

A shaman loses control of a spell. Ten people are killed, including the shaman. A witness says it looked as if the shaman had changed into something else the moment before the spell went out of control.

There were more.

Each told a similar tale.

I read them all, letting each slip to the floor until I stood there empty-handed. But there was still one more. I pulled it out. A letter from Dunkelzahn.

Aina,

In light of our last conversation, I thought these might be of interest to you. By the way, I've been keeping track of these things, and on the night you told me about, there was a spike at Crater Lake.

Dunkelzahn

I stayed there, staring off into space for a long time. Then suddenly I couldn't bear to stay inside any longer.

The sun was going down as I left the house. There

was a bit of a nip in the air. Winter had not yet completely let go. But I didn't feel the cold.

I felt numb. As though encased in amber. Fossilized.

Oh, what a fool I'd been. Thinking to protect them all from the Enemy. To warn them. What ego. What hubris.

For I knew now that I had done the very thing I'd warned them against.

I had used the power wantonly. Wastefully. And in so doing I'd made it easier for the Enemy to come across.

I realized now that Ysrthgrathe had sacrificed himself. His defeat was too easy. He'd played me. Played my emotions, manipulated me all along until I couldn't resist. It was his revenge. For he knew that nothing would bring me greater pain than to live with the knowledge that I'd had the means to stop them, and had let anger and fear and foolishness rule me instead.

My chest felt tight. There was nothing for me to do now but prepare. Prepare for that day which was as inevitable as death.

I stared up at the sky. The sun had set, yet a pale radiance still lingered. Then it began to rain. Black drops coming from a clear twilight sky.

I stayed there for a long time, letting the rain wash over me.

Author's Note

About a year and a half ago, I sent Sam Lewis, president of FASA, a sample of some of my writing. I sat on pins and needles for about three months, waiting for him to reply. Finally, I came home one day and there was a message on my answering machine from Sam: Liked what I read. Want to talk to you about a novel.

Sam was then, as he is now, a man of few words.

After I did a touchdown dance, I managed to pull myself together enough to call him back to discuss the matter in what (I hoped) was a cool and professional manner.

This event led to my writing not one, but three, novels for FASA.

The first two novels, *Scars* and *Little Treasures*, are set in the Earthdawn universe. The third novel, which you hold in your hands, was to be a Shadowrun crossover novel.

The three books are interconnected, but each can be read on its own. In each book, I tried to do something different with the characters. I won't tell you what happened in the Earthdawn books.

You'll just have to wait and read them for your-selves.

(Ooh, tough writer talk. Please buy them, huh?)

But *Worlds Without End* presented me with some unique challenges and opportunities.

I had to bring four of my characters forward almost six thousand years into the future. A very different future than they might have imagined. I had to think about what had happened among them during that time. And, most importantly, what did the immortal elves, or the Elders, do with themselves when the world was not replete with magic?

In writing *Worlds Without End,* I tried to imagine what it was that the Elders, the immortal elves of Shadowrun, did during the long years before the Awakening. Like any group of people, they would have different opinions on what their purpose was and how they should spend their talents. Of course there would be disagreements, love affairs, and political maneuvering among them.

And then there is the shared history of some of the immortals, from the time of Earthdawn. Earthdawn influences these immortals even when they themselves are not aware of it. The terrors of that time live in these Elders and have helped mold the spheres of their influence in Shadowrun.

Then it occurred to me that if *I* were immortal and had beaucoups power and probably wealth, I would get bored in a big hurry and probably end up messing about in all sorts of things that really weren't my business. Thus I decided that these immortals spent much of their time meddling in human history—both for good and ill.

The problem with this sort of thing, of course, is that the only people who can really appreciate it are other immortals. Not to mention the fact that they are the only people on the planet who share the same history and experience. As I grow older, I find this to be more and more an important factor in my life. A shared history.

After I managed to nail down the nature of the relationships, I then had to look into the established Shadowrun universe to see how to knit all of this together.

Aina spends the first half of *Worlds Without End* in Tír na nÓg. Much of her time is spent with the more mystical side of the Tír. This is due to the influence of the Seelie Court, the mystical center of this Tír. Matters of esoteric magical importance are dealt with here.

Other mystical elements at work in Tír na nÓg include the Doineann Draoidheil, for instance. This is a series of magical storms that rage across the cairn lines. This and the Veil are potent magical forces in this Tír, and I knew that this would be at work in Aina's reaction to the Tír.

Throughout the book, I tried to include real events, people, and folklore. For example, the each-uisge, a type of faerie creature, known for living in the bottom of lochs. It attacks unsuspecting victims, dragging them to the bottom of the loch where it then dines upon their flesh, spitting only the victims' livers up onto the shore.

Lovely creatures, these faerie folk.

I've often thought that fairy tales are both horrible and wonderful. Go mess with faery and you just might wake up and find yourself face to face with your great-grandchild with everyone you know long dead.

One final note: About mondegreens. I first learned what mondegreens were last year. Since I've been using them myself for years, it's good to know they have a name.

According to Jon Carroll, who uses the term in his book *Near Life Experiences,* "Mondegreens are the mishearing of the lyrics of popular songs, Christmas carols, hymns, patriotic affirmations, clichés—anything at all. The word 'mondegreen' was originally coined by the writer Sylvia Wright."

Mondegreens have popped up in other places. *Details* magazine ran a piece on them (though apparently didn't use the term mondegreen). Their best example is Billy Joel's "You may be Right."

Real lyric: "You may be right, I may be crazy." Mondegreen lyric: "You make the rice, I'll make the gravy."

Carroll likes one from Creedence Clearwater Revival's "Bad Moon Rising." Original lyric: "There's a bad moon on the rise." Mondegreen lyric: "There's a bathroom on the right."

Needless to say, such a cool thing had to show up in a book somewhere.

Love Long and Perspire.

—C. Spector, February 1995

Timeline

Following is a brief history of the events that shaped the world of 2056—the social and technological upheavals that have contributed to the awesome changes the Earth and her people have undergone over the past half-century. Changes no twentieth-century forecaster could ever have imagined.

2002

New technology makes it possible to construct the first optical chip that is proof against electromagnetic pulse effects.

2002-2008

The Resource Rush. United Oil and other major corporations demand and get licenses to exploit oil, mineral, and land resources on U.S. federal lands, including designated Indian lands. Radical Amerindians respond by forming the Sovereign American Indian Movement (SAIM).

2004

Libya unleashes a chemical weapon against Israel. Israel responds with a nuclear strike that destroys half of Libya's cities.

2005

A major earthquake in New York City kills more than 200,000 people, with damage at 20 million dollars. It will take 40 years to rebuild the city.

2006

Japan announces the creation of a new Japanese Imperial State. The Japanese deploy the first solar-powered collector satellites to beam microwave energy to receptors on the Earth's surface.

2009

Angry that the government has leased additional Indian lands to United Oil, SAIM commandos capture the Shiloh missile facility in Montana. All Amerindians occupying the facility are killed in a government raid. In the struggle, however, they launch a *Lone Eagle* missile toward the Russian Republic, bringing the world to the brink of nuclear war. The crisis ends when the warheads mysteriously fail to detonate.

2010

In retaliation for the Shiloh affair, the U.S. government passes the Re-Education and Relocation Act, authorizing the detention of thousands of Native Americans in concentration camps (euphemistically known as "Re-Education Centers").

First outbreak of Virally Induced Toxic Allergy Syndrome (VITAS), which kills 25 percent of the world's population before year's end.

2011

The Year of Chaos. Governments begin to topple, famine stalks the world, nuclear power plants suffer meltdown, with extensive radiation fallout.

The first mutant and changeling children are born, signaling the start of the UGE (Unexplained Genetic Expression) Syndrome. The news media dub these new beings as "elves" and "dwarfs."

On December 24, thousands of Japanese witness the first dragon, Ryumyo, reemerge from dormancy on Mt. Fuji. The same day, Daniel Howling Coyote leads his followers out of the Abilene Re-Education Center. He declares himself a shaman of the Great Ghost Dance, which involves powerful magic and promises to shatter the yoke of the white man once and for all.

Beginning in this year, political chaos begins to engulf the planet. The Federal government of Mexico dissolves in riots, while Tibet regains independence as magical defenses seal it off from invasion and render the region incommunicado. By the end of the year there is no question that magic has returned to the world.

2014

Ghost Dancers announce formation of the Native American Nations (NAN), with the Sovereign Tribal Council at its head. The Dancers claim responsibility for the eruption of Redondo Peak in New Mexico; Los Alamos is buried under a cloud of ash. A federal force sent in to retaliate is destroyed by tornadoes called down by the Ghost Dancers.

The United Free Republic of Ireland is established, while the white-controlled government of South Africa collapses.

2016

In a period of three weeks, U.S. President Jesse Garrety, Russian President Nikolai Chelenko, Prime Minister Lena Rodale of Great Britain, and Prime Minister Chaim Schon of Israel are assassinated. All but the Garrety assassin are killed in violent shootouts with local law officials.

2017

New U.S. President William Jarman issues the infamous Resolution Act, sanctioning the extermination of all Native American tribes. In response, Howling Coyote and his people begin the Great Ghost Dance. Freak weather and other uncanny events destroy or disrupt U.S. military bases slated for use in the genocidal plan. On August 17, Mount Hood, Mount Rainier, Mount St. Helens, and Mount Adams erupt simultaneously just as government troops are about to begin their attack. Former skeptics of the Dance begin to believe in its power.

2018

First-generation ASIST (Artificial Sensory Induction System Technology) is created by Dr. Hosato Hikita of ESP Systems in Chicago.

The Treaty of Denver is signed. With this agreement, the federal governments of the United States, Canada, and Mexico acknowledge the sovereignty of NAN over most of western North America. Seattle remains as an extraterritorial extension of the U.S. government in Native American lands.

The U.S. spaceplane *America,* with its secret military payload, disintegrates in orbit. The wreckage lands in Australia, killing 300 in the small town of Longreach.

2021

Goblinization. On April 30, 10 percent of the world's population suddenly begins to metamorphose into new racial types known today as orks and trolls. This transformation, popularly known as goblinization, marks another threshold point in the reemergence of magic on Earth. Humans react violently to the presence of the metahuman races in their midst.

Québec declares its independence, receiving immediate recognition from France.

2022

Severe rioting continues all over the world in response to the phenomenon of goblinization. The U.S. government declares martial law for several months, while reports trickling out of Russia indicate deaths on a mass scale. Many changed beings go into hiding or withdraw into separate communities.

Only another outbreak of VITAS quells the racial violence, leaving another 10 percent of the world's population dead in its wake.

The term "Awakened Beings" is coined to describe the metahumans and other emerging life forms.

2024

First simsense entertainment unit (a kind of sensory VCR) becomes available.

President Jarman is reelected U.S. President in a landslide victory based on the first use of the remote-vote system. Opposition parties claim fraud.

2025

Several prestigious U.S. universities establish the first undergraduate programs in occult studies.

2026

The U.S. Constitution is amended to include all metahumans.

The first cyberterminal (a room-sized isolation

chamber for a single operator) is developed. Funded by various intelligence agencies, the goal of the research is to make it possible for strike teams of "cybercommandos" to raid data systems.

2027

First commercial fusion reactor power plant comes on-line.

2028

In the United States, the CIA, NSA, and IRS pool their resources to recruit and train Echo Mirage, the first team of "cybercommandos."

2029

Computer Crash of '29. A mystery virus attacks databases worldwide, resulting in total financial chaos. The government and the megacorps attempt to fight the virus with their own cybercommandos, but eventually must recruit maverick hackers to fight the virus. In the course of fighting the virus and attempting to rebuild the world data system, the Matrix is born. The surviving hackers now have knowledge of cyberdecks and begin to cobble together their own units.

NAN declares that the emerging metahuman races are welcome in tribal lands.

2030

The remaining United States of America merges with Canada to form the United Canadian and

American States (UCAS). A coalition of southern states opposes the idea.

2030-2042

Euro-Wars. In this twelve-year period, Europe and Asia are rocked by a series of wars that result in a complete political transformation.

The European Economic Community collapses. Awakened species come to dominate vast wilderness areas, including portions of Siberia, Mongolia, and the mountains of northeastern China. In a return to city-state politics, Italy, southern France, and southeastern Europe fragment into hundreds of tiny sovereignties.

2034

A coup ousts President McGoldrick of Ireland. The coup was subtly masterminded by Liam O'Connor, whose Tir Republican Corps rose out of a dying IRA. Liam is asked to impose a state of emergency by acting President McCarthy. Liam uses this request to his advantage and creates a Tir out of Ireland: Tír na nÓg.

The first "gray market" cyberdecks become available.

The government of Brazil topples in the aftermath of an invasion by Awakened forces, including three dragons. The Awakened declare the new state of Amazonia.

A coalition of ten southern states secedes from UCAS to form the Confederated American States (CAS).

2035

The Elves of the Pacific Northwest secede from NAN, declaring themselves the nation of Tir Tairngire (Land of Promise) and confiscating Native American land for themselves. Violent clashes between Amerindian and elven tribes break out.

California declares independence from UCAS and is immediately recognized by Japan. Japanese land troops to protect their interests.

Texas secedes from CAS and makes an unsuccessful attempt to seize portions of southwestern Texas ceded to the tribes of Aztlan by the Treaty of Denver.

In 2035, the Tsimshian tribal coalition withdraws from NAN.

2036

A small community of Awakened beings in rural Ohio napalmed by Alamo 20,000, a terrorist group dedicated to destroying all Awakened beings. Over the next fifteen years, Alamo 20,000 is linked to the deaths of a thousand metahumans and openly sympathetic human supporters.

2037

First simsense entertainment unit introduced.

2039

Night of Rage. Racial violence breaks out in major urban centers of North America. Thousands die, most of them metahumans and their supporters.

2041

EuroAir Flight 329, en route from London to Atlanta, is destroyed over the Atlantic, killing all passengers and crew. Though garbled, the last transmission seems to indicate that the dragon Sirrurg attacked the craft. Many believe the flight was sabotaged to retaliate for the Night of Rage.

Policlubs, youth-oriented associations devoted to spreading various political or social philosophies, first appear in Europe. Each club hopes to recruit the masses to its own viewpoint and thus play a leading role in the European Restoration.

2043

Liam O'Connor, State President of Tír na nÓg, disappears. After Liam's disappearance his wife of two years, Brane Deigh, proclaims herself "Queen" of the Seelie Court, a non-legislative body said to influence the spirits of elves, rather than their minds or bodies.

Four chapters of the Universal Brotherhood, an organization espousing a philosophy based on EST, New Age pseudo-mysticism, and a healthy dose of Madison Avenue marketing smarts, open in California.

2044

Aztlan nationalizes all foreign-owned business. Semi-open war breaks out as some corporations fight to retain their holdings. Under cover of the fighting, Aztlan annexes most of what is left of Mexico except for the Yucatan, where Awakened forces halt all takeover attempts.

2045

A Universal Brotherhood branch opens in Seattle.

2046

The first simsense megahit, "Free Fall," starring Honey Brighton, eventually sells 50 million copies.

The policlub idea spreads to North America, but with violence in its wake. The Humanis Policlub, in particular, attracts a major following that cuts across economic, social, and political divisions. In a series of paid advertisements, Mothers of Metahumans (MOM) denounces Humanis as an arm of the shadowy Alamo 20,000.

2048

Tir Tairngire is admitted to the United Nations.

2049

The Governor of Seattle signs an exclusive trade deal with representatives of Tir Tairngire. Seattle, already a major cultural and economic center for the UCAS, NAN, and large segments of the Awakened, now takes on new importance as the only access to elven goods and services.

2050

The seventh-generation cyberdeck is introduced, now down to keyboard-size.

2051

The Universal Brotherhood now has over 400 chapters across the globe. Their members are predominately male, and predominately human. The Universal Brotherhood is secretly a front for a number of Insect totem hives.

2052

Major advances in cyber- and biotechnology. More and more humans and metahumans choose to enhance their bodies.

2055

Insect-spirits infest Chicago. The UCAS military detonates a subtactical nuclear weapon to destroy the primary hive, creating chaos as well as destruction. The military quarantines the city, sealing it off from the rest of the country.

2056

A Hawaiian nationalist group attempts to gain control of a magical site, intending to exploit the magic of the site to oust corps from Hawaii. Though their attempt fails, magic in the world spikes to a higher level.

Caroline Spector has written three computer game books, published through Prima Publishing (*Ultima: The Avatar Adventures, Ultima VII and Ultima Underworld: More Avatar Adventures,* and *The Might and Magic Compendium*). She has edited for *Amazing Stories* magazine and done freelance editing work for various publishers.

Worlds Without End is Spector's first published novel and is the third book in her **Immortals Trilogy**, which will continue with prequels *Scars* and *Little Treasures* to be published by FASA Corporation in 1996.

Coming Soon from ROC . . .

JUST COMPENSATION
by
Robert N. Charrette

NewsNet downline (04:04:31/8-13-55)
The Compensation Army

The occupation of the Federal District of Columbia by the so-called Compensation Expedition Force, or Compensation Army, begins its third month today. These homeless and forgotten "soldiers in the army of justice" have come to the Federal District to dramatize their long-ignored demands. The Army has come not to fight, but to lobby, to march, to form picket lines, and to insist that the compensation owed them be paid—and paid immediately.

Most of these soldiers are not warriors; they are just ordinary people who believe that they have been taken advantage of. The first to arrive in FDC were folk who had actually endured displacement from what are now the Native American Nations. These unfortunates were ousted from their homes and lands nearly forty years ago, when the old United States ceded most of its western states to the emerging and magically triumphant Native American Nations. Following the Treaty of Denver in 2018, the federal government promised compensation to the refugees. With the end of the old USA in 2036, the government of the new United Canadian and American States restricted those promises to all persons who originally resided in old US lands north of the 38th parallel, leaving the Confederated American States to care for the rest. Both US successor governments have denied restitution to any persons displaced from the now Free State of California.

Today's Comp Army is more than a few old men and women. Every day new "soldiers" arrive in the District—those already in the District are joined by friends, relatives, dependents, and sympathizers. The scattered tents and shanties have become a low-tech sprawl coating the FDC like a mold. Conditions in these makeshift communities are poor and growing poorer. The federal government issues promises, claiming that it is addressing the issue. Yet no real relief appears under way, and the mood among the Comp Army grows bleaker and more desperate.

Andy was a shadowrunner.

All his friends knew. He liked the way they looked impressed when he told them about his adventures. Except for Biddy Blackwell. Nothing much impressed Biddy.

This run was going to be one of the good ones; he could tell already from the way the meet was going. Mr. Johnson—not his real name, of course—was laying it out with just enough vagueness that Andy knew the story was pretty straight. When the details got real specific, it meant that the scam was on. Andy took in everything the Johnson laid out, filing it on his headware.

The Johnson said he represented a consortium of small businessmen trying to make it in the Anacostia Barrens. Brave souls—if they existed. Problem was, the Barrens were hotter than usual. The Halfies, top go-gang in the area, were rampaging. The go-gangers were thumping places up and down the Anacostia Barrens, everything from chop shops to clinics. The police were looking the other way—

standard—and the locals were terrified—also standard. Word was that somebody had stirred up the Halfies. Mr. Johnson wanted protection. He also wanted to know who was really responsible—and why they were doing it.

Johnsons were never what they said they were, but Andy took the job anyway. Being used to duplicity from employers, he retreated to his Appaloosa and set the autopilot to drive so that he could do other things.

The fixer from whom he'd gotten the Ferrari Appaloosa had said that it was "surplus," which for such a high-demand vehicle meant that it was hot. It was hot all right, and not just because it had been liberated from some military somewhere. Sheena the Appaloosa was the fastest armored vehicle on wheels. Street word said that wiz rigger Willie Williams swore by Appaloosas for high-threat runs, and now that he had one Andy understood why. The Appaloosa, with the custom shell that made Sheena look like a workhorse delivery truck rather than the thoroughbred predator that she was, had cost Andy just about all the cred he'd racked up from his last three runs. But she was worth it; jacked into Sheena's board, Andy could fight a small war or outrace just about any corp or FedPol pursuit car. Sheena was *meltdown* hot.

But he didn't need the Appaloosa's combat capabilities just now. No amount of real-world firepower meant drek in the Matrix; cyberspace had its own rules. But Andy was hot there, too. He started with turtle stuff, priming a herd of gophers and unleashing them on the media and public records. While they were hunting, Andy jacked and did a little direct prospecting in the FedPol database. He slipped past the outer IC shell with an ease and sleaze that would have impressed even FastJack. Not that cracking in was hard; the police department computers handled too much data to put it all behind serious IC, and the Intrusion Countermeasures protecting the incoming reports and complaints were light, little more than speedbumps for deckers of Andy's or FastJack's skills. Andy collected copies of every file on Halfie activities, dumped them into his bag, and flew back to his couch aboard Sheena to do a sort where he'd be safe from prying eyes or inadvertent discovery. Andy didn't like chance encounters in the Matrix; too much trouble and no reasonable expectation of gain.

Secure in the womb of the Appaloosa, Andy dumped his loot into a sorter. As the gophers came back, he added their finds. Monitoring the returns, he tweaked the search parameters as likely threads starting shaping up. The Johnson came back as a cipher—like *that* was a surprise?—so Andy looked for connections among the Halfies' targets. Mr. Johnson's interests should show up there. All Andy would have to do was recognize them.

There were chopshops on the target list, and that didn't fit with the Halfies' interests. Street word said that they controlled most of the shops in the barrens. Why hit your own income sources? As a cover, maybe. There was no doubt that the Halfies were spreading their good cheer around, but they seemed to be thumping some targets harder than others. How bad were the chopshops hit? Not bad at all. The cover theory was starting to look good. So who was taking it on the chin the hardest? A quick sort by level of damage turned up a list that had a lot of free clinics and doc-in-a-boxes on it. Real nest-fouling stuff to trash the local medical care, and not like the territorial Halfies at all. A closer look showed that the go-gangers' choice of clinics wasn't random; for example, not a single DocWagon operation had been thumped. Andy scented a clue and popped into cyberspace to run down a few leads. He came back with the connection he was looking for: all the wrecked clinics either were sponsored by or ran programs funded by Biotechnics, the genengineering and pharmaceutical multinational. A quick check of media databases showed no similar rash of attacks on Biotechnics clinics in any other cities. What made the Anacostia clinics different? Andy bet that Mr. Johnson, or his bosses, knew. A direct Matrix run against Biotechnics was contraindicated just yet, so Andy picked a thumped clinic at random and went after its files, looking for anything unusual. He found records for three test programs. A second clinic's records only held one match: a drug treatment pilot program for something called Azadone, trademark still pending. It was a conclusion-jump, but Andy felt sure that Azadone was at the heart of Mr. Johnson's concerns. He'd check it out later.

Right now, Sheena was beeping that they had

nearly reached their destination. That was fine by Andy. He switched jacks and took over Sheena's control. This run wasn't going to be solved with just a little Matrix hacking. They never were. That also was fine by Andy; he liked a good mix of action. It was time to move on to the next step. He nosed the Appaloosa into the first available parking spot after he crossed Maple Avenue.

"Take care of yourself, Sheena," he told the Appaloosa as he dismounted, activating her anti-theft routines. Fairfax wasn't the worst of the District's regions, but this wasn't the best part of Fairfax. Even if you didn't know that from previous experience the way Andy did, you could see it in the unrepaired streetlights, the graffiti-covered walls, and the boarded-over storefronts.

The night outside the Appaloosa held no secrets from him, because his eyes were Telestrian Cyberdyne 48's, built under license from Zeiss. They were not the latest model, but then cybereye technology hadn't advanced much in the past ten years. The 48's weren't fully-featured either; they didn't have the full thermal imaging package, just ambient light amplification. But that was more than enough to pierce the gloom of Old Courthouse Road and note each and every one of the derelicts and streetrats huddling in the doorways and skulking in the alleys. All locals he'd seen before; they would know his rep and wouldn't bother him.

His team was waiting for him at Eskimo Nell's, their usual watering hole and gathering place. There were just two today, Buckhead and Feather; he didn't figure he'd need more. Buckhead was muscle, simple but not cheap. The ork was very, very good at what he did, but all of his personality was in his cyberware and his guns. Feather was an elf and a mage, and her style of dress was more suited to *'Runner Babes* than to real shadowrunning, but what she wore—or rather, didn't wear—didn't affect her performance, so what was there to say? Besides, Andy enjoyed looking at her.

"Hoi, Boss. Whuzzappening?" It was Buckhead's standard opening line.

Andy dove right in and told them about the job he'd taken for them, and about his theory that the clinics were the focus of the violence. "We're reactive protection, but we're also supposed to find out who's behind it."

"What makes Johnson think dat all the thumpin' ain't just boys 'n girls out ta have fun?"

"You can't think that the patients and staff at the clinics are having fun," Feather said.

"We need to make a move," Andy said. He wasn't in the mood for sitting around and hashing out the possibilities. Andy and his runners needed a connection and their best bet lay with the Halfies. Who would know better than the go-gangers why they were thumping their way through the Barrens? "I think we should go have a chat with some Halfies."

"I know one of their squats," Feather said, surprising Andy.

He knew that she had a lot of street connections, but he hadn't figured on her knowing much about go-gangs. He was quite happy to be wrong. "Let's roll, then."

Following Feather's directions, Andy piloted the Appaloosa across the river and out into the fringes of the Anacostia Barrens. Andy drove slowly, because of the road conditions as much as the need to recon. They scouted the old poured concrete building that Feather led them to, and determined that some of the go-gangers were home; it was still early for them to be out raising hell. The place was solidly built, probably why the gangers laired there. Whatever it had once been, it sported a pair of vehicle doors on one side. The only human door was on that side, too. Andy decided on the direct approach, and put the Sheena's nose through the flimsy corrugated plastic of the left garage door. The building wall would cover their left flank.

Buckhead exited the Appaloosa with a whoop. Feather was quieter, but no less eager. Arcane energy raised her hair in a crackly static halo that would be a fright to see coming at you. Andy almost felt sorry for the scrambling Halfies—at least one of whom had literally been caught with his pants down.

Once he'd used Sheena to crack open the Halfies' squat, Andy was willing to let Buckhead and Feather take care of the gangers. He could have gotten involved, but combat wasn't his thing. He didn't get a jolt from it like some people did. He'd step in if he had to, but he didn't think that would be necessary. He had a good team and the opposition this early in the run wasn't likely to be anything that they couldn't handle.

"We need a talker," Andy reminded his team over the commlink. There was no acknowledgment, but when the ruckus died down, Buckhead and Feather returned with one of the gangers.

"We could turn him over to the police," Feather suggested. She had a tendency to offer the law-abiding solution. Andy figured it was just so that he'd know there was one. "The FedPols will be happy to see him. Of course, if he tells us what we want to know . . ."

"I ain't talking," the Halfie said. The black pigmentation on the upper half of his face almost hid his frown of determination.

"I can make him talk," Buckhead said. The ork slid his paired chrome spurs in and out of their wrist sheaths to demonstrate the method he intended to employ. It was nasty, but it might get them fast results. Life in the shadows wasn't nice.

"Okay," Andy said, "but try and keep him quiet."

The Halfie had known he was living dangerously when he took money to go thumping innocents.

Buckhead grinned and led the Halfie away. In an elapsed time of twenty minutes, exactly, he came back with an address. The address supposedly belonged to a middleman.

Andy and the team paid the guy a visit, and he proved to be surprisingly reasonable. For a fee—that Andy would list as an expense when he billed Mr. Johnson—the fixer confirmed the Halfie's story about a simple violence-for-hire gig. The fixer couldn't confirm the power behind the job in spite of Andy's offer to double the fee, which lent credibility to the man's claim. Yet for another fee, the fixer offered them a cryptic clue. "Wanna see who's casting shadow? Drive Wisconsin and drop anchor six south of the cathedral."

They followed the directions.

Andy remembered the building as being the offices of Micronetics, a Saeder-Krupp subsidiary, but a throbbing neon sign proclaimed it the property of Vilanni Corp. Whenever he hit such a change, he reminded himself of just how fast things changed in the corporate world. More often than not, today's hot comer was tomorrow's washed-up loser.

The Vilanni name wasn't new to him. He'd crossed paths with them before, and he knew that the corp was about as underhanded as they came. Andy didn't think them above trashing clinics just to ruin a competitor's market test. The thought of ruining test markets reminded him of Vinton and the Hanging File Run. The sort of thing going down in the Barrens was just Vinton's style.

But Andy's hunch and a fixer's hint that Vilanni was behind everything wouldn't be enough for his employer. Andy needed to come up with a convincing connection. There was also the little matter of determining *why* Vilanni was involved. No Johnson was ever satisfied without knowing why he'd been targeted.

Word about their hit against the Halfies would be filtering up the food chain. There would be no better time for a fast run against the Vilanni mainframe. He put them a dozen blocks down Wisconsin and onto one of the quiet, narrow side streets of Georgetown before parking the Appaloosa and jacking in.

The Vilanni mainframe showed as a black monolith in cyberspace. It was a tough nut, but Andy knew better than to come at it head on. He tried something new, running a side program to jigger things a bit. With effortless precision he focused in on a small section of the monolith, narrowing his perception until pits on the black surface grew to pocks, then holes, and finally tunnels. He'd used one of those tunnels before, a back door set by a renegade Vilanni programmer. Since he'd used it in the Hanging File Run, the entry should have been locked and sealed, but he was pleased to see that the tinkering that he'd done had worked. The door remained operable. Inside, he zoomed to Vinton's private space and started nosing around the Vilanni exec's files. It wasn't long before he struck paydata: a list of clinics, Biotechnics clinics.

While he was checking out the list, a time-date stamp clicked next to one of them. That was the cue for the file to activate a slave routine. Andy scoped the program. Somewhere in Vilanni HQ, a call was being made. Andy slapped a tag on it just before the connection broke. He kept digging while he waited for the tag to come back. He hadn't managed to find anything juicy by the time it returned, trailing a string of connections that were more than enough to cut out a tag that lacked the advantage of getting on board at the start. The final destination of the call was in the Anacostia Barrens, and all the tag's message-backfeed feature held was the address of the clinic and a time-date stamp—the same as the one on the list. Andy had discovered the time and place of the next thump.

It was decision time. Did he cut short his run against the Vilanni mainframe and lead his team in an intercept of the thump that was about to go down, or did he stay in the system to take advantage of his penetration and go after incriminating evidence that would put an end to all of the thumps? If he pulled out, the system would be tougher to crack when he got back— but if he didn't, people would be hurt, maybe killed. Then again, more would be hurt and killed if he didn't get what he needed out of the Vilanni mainframe, and he might not get this good a chance again.

The datastore's walls shimmered and a crystalline spider oozed through—Vilanni IC had found him. First things first. He engaged his Claw Hand attack program. The battle against the IC was short and sharp, but the outcome was never in doubt. Maybe FastJack could have taken the spider down quicker. Maybe.

But the spider was just the first of Vilanni's defenses. There would be worse soon.

FLASH!

Cyberspace around him winked from its normal image to a negative version.

Sooner than soon.

FLASH!

Damn! Not now? Clearly, he'd lost track of time. There was nothing else he could do now but bail. He'd be hosed if he didn't get out.

▼ 14 ▼
NOSFERATU
by Carl Sargent and Marc Gascoigne

NOWHERE TO HIDE

Elf Serrin Shamandar, rootless mage and part-time shadowrunner, is on the run. Somebody is determined to corner him—he doesn't know who or why. With help from Michael Sutherland, a brilliant decker, and a troll-samurai named Tom, Serrin manages to stay one step ahead of his unseen enemy. Kristin, a street kid from Capetown with an extensive list of names, or victims, to her credit is not making that easy.

Everywhere they go they feel evil eyes, *elven eyes,* watching them. As they gradually learn of their enemy's plan to wipe humanity off the face of the planet, Serrin and his friends become desperate to confront him. Their enemy, however, is in no such hurry. Why should he be? Relentless, powerful, demonic, hasn't he already been waiting for more than three hundred years . . . ?

▼ 15 ▼
BURNING BRIGHT
by Tom Dowd

THE BREEDING IS COMPLETE

Mitch Truman, young heir to an entertainment megacorp, is missing. Maybe he ran off with the woman he loves. But when it becomes evident some major insect magic is involved, the reason becomes far far darker.

Dan Truman, CEO of the media giant Truman Technologies, doesn't care about the dangers—he just wants his son back. Price is no object, neither is propriety. He'll only hire the best to find Mitch, even if their motives are suspect.

Kyle Teller is the best. He's done this job before. He's experienced. Finding the boy will be a cinch. Except . . . there's something Kyle doesn't know.

He's about to find out.

All the money and experience in the world may not be enough to defeat the terrible parasitic Power multiplying under the city of Chicago.

▼ 16 ▼
WHO HUNTS THE HUNTER
by Nyx Smith

HUNTER AND HUNTED

From the distant forests of Maine comes the deadly Weretiger known as Striper, seeking nature's own special justice—a mother's vengeance.

From the shadowed heart of the South Bronx comes the shaman known as Bandit, interested only in the pursuit of arcane arts and the reconciliation with nature his totem Racoon demands.

From the nightmare streets of Newark come Monk and Minx, seeking Life itself.

And from a corporate Laboratory comes a dark, desperate horror.

Who is predator and who is prey? The assassin? The shaman? The kids with the red flashing eyes? The Director of Resources at the Hurley-Cooper Labs, or HCL's dedicated scientists? Is it the criminal elves? Or the mysterious man from the Department of Water and Wastewater Management with a technical rating even higher than God's?

Before they are done, a killer will learn the meaning of mercy, and one who honored life will discover the necessity of ruthless destruction . . .

HOUSE OF THE SUN
by Nigel Findley

DIRK MONTGOMERY IS BACK

Dirk Montgomery, former Lone Star cop turned shadowrunner, knows the shadowy byways of Seattle and the Amerind city of Cheyenne.

He knows when to take chances and when to take cover.

He knows the rules of the game that is survival.

But when a megacorp exec demands payment of an old debt, Dirk finds himself in an environment where the old rules don't apply anymore.

To some the Kingdom of Hawai'i is a tropical playground . . . but it has a sinister underside. It's this underside Dirk must navigate as he tries to stay one step ahead of the factions competing for control of the islands: the megacorps, the government, the rebels and the yakuza, plus dragons, elves, new friends . . . and old enemies.

COMING IN JANUARY 1996

▼ 19 ▼
JUST COMPENSATION
by Robert Charrette

DEECEE IS BURNING!

Andy was happy as a shadowrunner wannabe, but when he accidentally gets involved with real runners, the game of let's pretend is over. So is his safe, corporate life.

Andy's half-brother, UCAS Army Major Tom Rocquette, has some doubts about what he's involved with too. Why, for example, is he being ordered to mercilessly massacre the Compensation Army, a group that, like him, only seeks justice?

Andy and Tom, along with runners Markowitz and Kit, are finding out things it'd be safer not to know. Things that put many lives in danger and point to a sinister web of dirty politicians, dishonorable officers, and misused tech and magic—a conspiracy to dismantle the entire UCAS government!

Can they find enough evidence to stop it before the nation's capitol is buried under a heap of bloody corpses?!

▼ **20** ▼
BLACK MADONNA
by Carl Sargent and
Marc Gascoigne

MONA LISA SMILES

Leo is a bit strange. He's also one of the most brilliant scientific and artistic minds operating on the planet. His dream is to build a Great Laboratory for artists, scientists and genius-types such as himself. His dream is to tell the world the Real Truth. And this is one immortal elf who knows what it is.

The only problem is Leo doesn't have any money. But corps have money. So, Leo simply stages the most stylish and sophisticated electronic blackmail ever perpetrated—targeting every major megacorp on the globe.

When Renraku Corp hires out elven mage Serrin Shamandar and decker Michael Sutherland to find Leo, it soon becomes obvious they are searching for more than an ordinary hacker, and more than an ordinary man.

The corps aren't the only ones who want to get their hands on Leo. The Vatican and the occult Priory of Sion also possess Leo's secret knowledge, but they don't want to share it with the world. In fact they don't want Leo sharing it either. In fact, they want Leo dead.

What is this truth? Is the world ready for it?

Or will the world just laugh?

FASA

RELENTLESS ACTION FROM BATTLETECH ®

YOUR OPINION CAN MAKE A DIFFERENCE!

LET US KNOW WHAT *YOU* THINK.

Send this completed survey to us and enter a weekly drawing to win a special prize!

1.) Do you play any of the following role-playing games?
Shadowrun _____ Earthdawn _____ BattleTech _____

2.) Did you play any of the games before you read the novels?
Yes _____ No _____

3.) How many novels have you read in each of the following series?
Shadowrun _____ Earthdawn _____ BattleTech _____

4.) What other game novel lines do you read?
TSR _____ White Wolf _____ Other (Specify) _____

5.) Who is your favorite FASA author?
_____

6.) Which book did you take this survey from?
_____

7.) Where did you buy this book?
Bookstore _____ Game Store _____ Comic Store _____
FASA Mail Order _____ Other (Specify) _____

8.) Your opinion of the book (please print)
_____
_____
_____

Name _____ Age _____ Gender _____
Address _____
City _____ State ____ Country _____ Zip _____

Send this page or a photocopy of it to:
FASA Corporation
Editorial/Novels
1100 W. Cermak Suite B-305
Chicago, IL 60608